THE SUCCESS
OF FAILURE

THE SUCCESS OF FAILURE

THE MYSTERIOUS BILLIONAIRE PLAN

David Singer with Don Friend

ISBN: 0999822403
ISBN 13: 9780999822401
Library of Congress Control Number: 2018900759

TABLE OF CONTENTS

CHAPTER 1

HONG KONG

"Hello, Pierce, this is Pricilla Chong. I need to meet with you right away. This is a matter that I cannot discuss over the phone."

The streets of Hong Kong were choked with traffic, but her limousine filtered through it smoothly. It went to Tsim She Tsui on the waterfront, a beautiful townhouse with no signage. Discretion was one of Pierce's most important assets. His investigations were of the highest level and delicately handled. His outcomes were something Pricilla had counted upon before. As she approached the front door, she was greeted by the man himself. Her family and their vast fortune were legendary in Hong Kong.

Pricilla looked like a model prepared for a shoot. Her gait was smooth and luxurious as she entered his office. Her Eurasian features were soft and radiant. The only sign that something was off that his trained eye could discern was a stressed look around her mouth.

"Time is valuable, and in this situation I have precious little of it. My father is infatuated with a woman, and I believe that it is serious. There is a great disparity in their ages, but he is very happy. I wouldn't mind if I didn't have a very strange feeling about her. She is mysterious and exotic, but something about her makes me very uncomfortable."

As was his professional training, Pierce Lee listened with insightful perception. Since her mother had died four years ago, Pricilla was very protective of and focused on her father. Was this a jealous reaction on her part, or was there something to be concerned about? The artful skill of questioning would be the first step to determine if there was cause for concern. "Tell me everything you know, starting with how your father met her. Is she Chinese; how old is she? Is she educated? What is her name?"

Pricilla sat down in the very worn but comfortable sofa and admitted that everything was mysterious about her. All she knew was that her first name was Loana and that since she appeared in her father's life, he had regained his will to live. Since then he has become a happy man. Now he talks about his future projects and objectives. I want to be sure that she is for real and not someone who suddenly appeared in his life with an ulterior plan of some kind.

Pricilla slumped into the sofa, her soft yellow blouse contrasting with her bronze skin tone. Her eyes slowly focused on Pierce, ready for some answers but knowing that now there would only be questions. She reviewed the recent past in her mind. Where could she begin?

Sensing that she was lost in thought, Pierce gently said, "When and where did they meet?"

In a flash she could recall the scene. She had encouraged her father to order some new clothes, and the tailor arrived at the house with samples and to take measurements. She had pushed him because he had been obviously depressed since the loss of his wife of forty-four years. This young, beautiful woman had entered their home as the tailor's assistant. She was slender and shapely, with an unusual look. She had long black hair pulled severely to one side. Her clothes were tapered, and her form was muscular and chiseled. Her tanned skin glistened with youthful sensuality. Upon their meeting, her father smiled, something he had not done in a long time. When she spoke, her accent rounded out the words into smooth sounds. Pricilla recalled that she was so happy to see her father smile, she initially thought that it had to do with the selections of new shirts, slacks, and suits that were in progress. Little did she know that her life and her father's life were about to change profoundly.

She told Pierce the little she knew, and let him start to delve in a way that reflected his expertise. In the past he had demonstrated his ability to uncover facts that were hidden in plain sight. They spoke briefly, and he promised to advise her on the outcome of the investigation. She left the room and suddenly returned to let him know that he had carte blanche in expenses. "Do whatever is necessary to investigate, but under no circumstances can she find out that I have initiated this investigation."

Pierce had a worldwide organization—he had offices in most major cities in the world—but kept his headquarters in his birth city, Hong Kong. He immediately put his people on this case, and in less than an hour, they had the following information: Her name was Loana Wood, born in Bistriţa, Romania, age twenty-three. She had entered Hong Kong via Heathrow a month ago and was temporarily employed at the Ritz-Carlton Hotel on Austin Road West. She began as a hotel maid and surprisingly, one week after, was ascended to a high-paying job in the public-relations department. On the day she met Pricilla's father, she had come with the custom tailor to assist him in the clothes-selection process. The hotel responded gingerly to his call because of his importance in the Hong Kong financial community. Upon closer look at her passport, one of the detectives noticed some irregularities that they would check out. Pierce also sent men to Romania and London to investigate her more thoroughly.

It was evident to Miss Chong that she had chosen the right person to investigate this. Her curiosity and worry grew as the days passed, and she called Pierce for an update. In this interim report, he shared that upon arrival in Hong Kong, she registered as a tourist but went directly to the hotel, where one of the employees procured her the maid's job. Her ability to speak English was poor, but utilizing her intellect she made herself understood. She was so attractive that whoever met her saw only the totality of her striking beauty. Her movement exuded sensuality, and both men women were hypnotized by her presentation of self. A week later she met the public-relations manager, and he insisted she work in his department. A few days later, she accompanied the tailor to present the fabrics for clothes for your father. That's how your father met her.

"My people in Romania went to Bucharest and have made little progress so far. It seems that there is a lot of corruption, but money talks, and we should get some information soon. As far as my men in London, they have traced the name Loana Wood but found over six hundred women with the same name. I gave them some time to find out the possible connection to our Loana."

"How did you find her passport?" Pricilla asked.

"Well, since she lives and works in the hotel, we have a contact that was able to get it for us. Then I had one of my legal-document associates look it over. We also found that she only had two changes of clothes and no other ID. Oh, yes, and my men found a diary written in Romanian, and we sent a copy to our linguist for translation and information. We took note of the fact that all her cosmetics and wash items were new, and her travel bag was very deteriorated and totally different from all her other belongings. When attempting to find out who gave her the maid's job at the hotel, we were told that it was through one of the butlers. He is a Romanian, with a Gypsy background, and he told our investigator, 'We Gypsies help each other; she came to me with a letter from my cousin, introducing her as a beautiful Gypsy relative. She was so beautiful and sexy that I couldn't refuse, and I got her a job. Why do you ask? Loana was promoted immediately by my superiors. She is top of the line. All Gypsies are top of the line. Another of her assets is that she speaks Romani—a Gypsy language—Romanian, a little English, and also told me she had learned some Mandarin.'"

CHAPTER 2

INSPIRATION

I t was Sunday afternoon, and Matei Wood was in a hurry. He had to close his shop early since his son, Constantin, was arriving from Bucharest with a definite plan. He summoned his wife and three daughters. His wife had prepared an incredible meal of *mititei* and *mamilige* with *sarmale* (cabbage rolls)—those were the favorite foods of all his children.

To be honest, I haven't slept well in months. My girls are coming of an age when all the young available men in town want to take them as wives. I have done the impossible and avoided them getting involved with our local boys. That is a difficult task since they are so beautiful. But I have to do something to get them out of here. My grandfather and my father were burdened by extreme poverty. I am the first who has a shop, but still we barely survive. My children have to leave this part of the world to prosper; that is my objective in life. I sent Constantin, my only boy, to study in Bucharest. He is a good and smart son, and he says he has a good plan for his sisters. I want to hear what it is.

Matei knew that his Gypsy ancestors were considered evil, cunning, mysterious outsiders. Some of the many Gypsy groups were wonderers; they moved from one area of Europe to the other, never establishing themselves. They were feared and stereotyped as being dishonest and mischievous. They were unfairly accused of stealing and betrayal. No, no. I don't want this for my children. I will save them from this horrible perception of our people.

Matei's oldest child was Constantin who was a very good-looking young man. He had a good and wholesome face, not ethnically identified. This, combined with his tremendous personality and his natural ability to be a leader, made him special. His father, Matei, had made an extraordinary effort to send him to a private school in Romania's capital, Bucharest. He was accepted mainly because of his presentation, verbal skills, and leadership qualities. Unfortunately, his education in the schools of his town was mediocre. Superior schools required a lot more. Luck came his way when he met another student, Dimitru, before his interview. Dimitru instantly became his friend and benefactor. This young man came from an extremely wealthy Romanian family. His family owned miles and miles of land with oil beneath it. After a few minutes of conversation, Dimitru felt like a kindred spirit, and he invited his newfound friend to his home. Constantin was able to stay there for the two years that he was in Bucharest. Armed with Dimitru's families support and recommendation, he was accepted to the Polytechnic University, one of the best academic institutions, if not the best, in Bucharest.

Constantin studied very hard, and it was very difficult for him. He lacked the basic background, but Dimitru helped him, and so did many of his fellow students. There was no doubt that his leadership qualities and incredible personality pushed him forward. During those two years of school, he lived in a rich man's house and only mingled with very cultured students. All this gave him the knowledge and culture that he had been lacking for the larger world that he wished to enter. On one occasion, Dimitru's family invited him for a weekend in London and arranged a passport for him. They all flew to Heathrow. Since this was his first flight, it was a little scary. He soon overcame his fear and learned a lot. He experienced flying, its customs, immigration process, and airports in general. The experience of visiting such a big, diverse, incredible city gave him even greater inspiration, and he started to devise a plan. This was to be the beginning of how he would rescue his three sisters, and his parents, from the continuation of his family's miserable life.

CHAPTER 3

KINDRED SPIRITS

Dimitru was a tall thin, handsome young man. Though he was born into a very wealthy family by the time he was in High School he had not developed any very close friendships. He received the best education available in his country and always received the highest grades in his academic work. He was competitive and aggressive and as a result he was a loner. It was an environment that pitted each student against everyone else. He always suspected they befriended him because of his wealth or for an academic advantage. Yet, all the females were always after him, and they wanted to take advantage of his popularity and position in the student body. He tended to avoid the other male students in his high school. At the interview for the Polytechnic Institute, he'd met Constantin in the waiting room. They had a long conversation while waiting to be interviewed. In that contact Dimitru saw different qualities in this new student. There was something unique about him, and strangely Dimitru felt that they were going to be great friends. This was such a different type of person, one that Dimitru could easily relate to. Constantin reflected the attitude that he was independent, a young man from a more limited background, but yet he was striving and forging a life plan. For both young men things were going to be different now.

Dimitru had graduated high school with the intention of studying computer engineering. He hoped to be accepted to Georgia Tech, Stanford or MIT. There was pressure from his parents to remain at home and continue his studies from there. He was their only son, and they wanted him to be close by. Suddenly there was a new incentive to stay at home, his new friend Constantin. Dimitru realized that Constantin needed help. Dimitru's noble purpose had been found adding a new dimension to his life. The mission he took on was getting Constantin into the Technological Institute, and thereby promoting their friendship. In service of keeping him at home, he was sure his parents would accept sponsoring a less-advantaged student whom he wished to befriend. There was more to Constantin than met the eye. He seemed to be a young man who had a definite life plan. Since Dimitru's future was unclear, it was amazing to him that Constantin seemed so driven and organized. These qualities caused Dimitru to stop and examine his loose plan to go to the United States to study. Suddenly, he found a cause, Constantin. They both discussed plans for the future, and Dimitru knew that he could obtain easy entrance for both himself and Constantin, with his father's influence.

After their interview Dimitru invited him to a nearby bar to get to know each other better. Over drinks, they continued their conversation. There, Dimitru ordered a slivovitz, as had become his habit, but Constantin refrained, and ordered a soft drink. Dimitru commented, "Here in Bucharest the price of a soft drink is eighty-seven percent of the price of slivovitz, but I prefer slivovitz!"

Constantin replied in the blink of an eye. "In every seven and three-fourths drinks, I get an extra one!" Dimitru was amazed at the speed and accuracy of his computation. Both young men were highly proficient in mathematics, and this was their first math encounter. Now Dimitru knew that he had found a basis for his father to get Constantin into the institute. As the conversation continued, a very attractive woman entered the bar. They caught a glimpse of her, and both commented on her physical attributes. They realized that a new chapter was about to start in both their lives relating to women. Constantin had been warned by his father that there were severe consequences for unprotected sex, but in Bistriţa, who could afford a prophylactic? This would be one trap in life that he could avoid by abstinence. Being a young handsome man, Constantin found this was a tough rule to follow, but he followed it.

Constantin was very impressed with his new friend. This Dimitru appeared as if by magic, and it was like a fairy tale come true. A really great educated, charming, athletic, intelligent, and wealthy man just became my friend. Now it seems that he wants to be my benefactor also. I had found a room to rent that I could afford near the institute. That same day, the interview went well. However, when I was told of the tuition requirements, I gave up hope. I figured I would need to get a job doing anything so that I could survive. I would need to save some money first to begin a life in Bucharest. Maybe, if I was lucky and played the lottery, I would have a chance of paying the tuition. My mother's advice to me had been, "Use my lucky numbers, and you will win." I happen to know that all Gypsies do is base winning on luck and numbers and dreams. I guess that in the situation I am in right now, there is little else to do but dream of a miracle. The miracle did not happen with the lottery; the miracle happened when I met Dimitru. He came over early the next day to tell me that he had spoken to his parents. They had agreed to all his reasoning as to why he wanted to help me and how he would help me. Mr. Agnelli, his father, would definitely take care of my admission and tuition. He also had influence with the board of directors at the institute".

"After I explained my need to have a friend around, and especially one who needs financial help, my parents agreed to have you move to their house temporarily, until you organize your life, Constantin. I was so happy I could hardly sleep, and now I am here to help you move into my house."

Constantin was astonished at all the news he had just been given. He didn't know the proper way of responding, so all he did was hug his newfound benefactor. Gypsy luck, he thought, had just become reality.

Life was treating him incredibly well. This was the third

month living in Bucharest. He was living in a superluxurious house and had met a fantastic family who accepted him like a son. Dimitru had gone shopping with him and bought him very expensive modern clothes. Now he felt like a new Constantin, one who fit into Bucharest society. He had been accepted to the institute because of the Agnellis. He had been very lucky to blend in perfectly with the other students. His ability to achieve the highest grades in his math classes and a willingness to work hard to catch up in other academic areas was a formula for success. He was well liked, and no one knew his real origins. Constantin was not ashamed of his Gypsy background, but he now felt that he had surpassed what could have been a barrier of culture. This institute offered access to education that did not exist for, or was simply not expected of, people of Gypsy origin. The differences were clear to him when he remembered back and compared his current learning to what was available in his old neighborhood. During his free time, he practiced soccer with Dimitru, and both of them proved to be very good in Romania's number-one sport. One evening while they both prepared for a physics exam, Dimitru brought up the money matter. He mentioned that he had a personal savings account that had been set up by his deceased grandfather. Now to make Constantin's life easier, he would lend him whatever was necessary to live better. In this way, Constantin could accept social invitations along with him and start dating some of the girls they both seemed to attract. He told Constantin, "Keep a record of everything I have loaned you from the beginning. I am sure you will return everything in the future. I trust you." That was something Dimitru continuously said. Constantin would answer, "I also trust you, Dimitru." Months went by, and their trust increased. Both young men often said, "You feel like a brother to me." Strangely, the Agnellis viewed him as another son and when they planned a family trip to London, there was no question that Constantin would accompany them.

CHAPTER 4

DIFFERENT PATHS TAKEN

The first night Constantin and Dimitru were in London, they ate with the family in a marvelous restaurant, and then they decided to explore the nightlife in the area. They were directed by the hotel concierge to visit a specific area where there were bars and music. They entered one of the bars, attracted by the noise, music, and laughter.

In a few minutes, they were approached by two young women looking for men and fun. Though Constantin was unfamiliar with the dances, he moved with the music. The woman started to talk, and he noticed her accent seemed to be Romanian. He spoke to her in Romanian, and she was startled by this. After a few moments, she explained that she wanted to take him to the rooms in the back of the bar, and he accepted. They went into a shabby room with a bed and nothing else. She started fondling him, took off her clothes, and immediately attempted to undress him. He was confused by all this sudden and unexpected behavior. After all he was a man, and she was a very sexy lady with beautiful breasts and an incredible figure. But he stopped her and said, "Wait a minute. What is this? Are you a prostitute? What are your intentions?"

She began to cry, sat down, and started to tell him why she was doing this so fast and with no foreplay. She had a quota of six men per night, and she was never going to be able to reach six men that night. He asked her how much she expected him to pay, and he paid her. Then he told her to get dressed. He asked her to meet him the next morning in a nearby park. He promised to listen to her dilemma and see what he could do to help her.

When he arrived the next day, she was there waiting. He noticed she was very pretty, and she reminded him of one of his sisters. She looked seventeen, he thought. She started explaining that a year ago a man came to her town in Romania, promising jobs. He said she would live in London with ability to make a lot of money. She could send back money to her impoverished family. He gave each family a down payment of €500, which is a fortune in a poor area. A whole line of girls came to be interviewed. He selected the twenty-five most attractive young woman and promised their families that they would soon be wealthy. The girl continued to say that he got them passports. Inside of a week's time, they were in London, all crammed into two rooms of a tiny apartment.

"He and an elderly woman started to teach us some words and phrases in English. They gave us junk food every day. Then one by one we were taken to different hotels to be maids. It was a lot of work and almost no pay. Three months later a man came up to me and offered me one hundred English pounds a day to work in a bar. This sounded great, and I immediately accepted. He paid the original man who brought me to London five thousand euros so I could leave. I didn't realize then that I had been sold! In no time they forced me into prostitution and they send my family one hundred euros a month. Meanwhile, I live a horrible life, and so do all the girls I know. I only have one night off a week, and I don't know anyone here in London. All the girls are in the same situation, and we are from various countries. They took our passports away, so we can't leave, go back, or go to the police. Can you help me?"

He told her that he would like to help her but didn't know how. He took down the telephone number of the bar she worked and lived in.

CHAPTER 5

CONSTANTIN BEGINS TO UNDERSTAND THE KEY TO A BETTER LIFE

Constantin couldn't sleep at all that night. All was clear to him. All he thought about was his promise to his father that his sisters would not remain in Bistriţa. They would not live with the poverty and misery that all Gypsy families were prone to. This was not going to happen to his family. Sending them overseas somewhere might convert them into low-class workers or lead them into prostitution. He had to devise a plan that would work and that would guarantee his sisters would prosper. Then they could help their parents leave the slums of their town and live like normal citizens. In Bucharest, he saw what a normal family looked like, and now in his brief visit to London, he saw how wonderful everything could be. He went to bathrooms that were clean and modern; he saw kitchens and refrigerators full of food. This was not what was happening in his home or any of the homes in his area. Poverty caused people to hunt for the food they needed every day.

As Constantin reflected on his past life he thought; *at home we would eat a meager meal; that's why we were all skinny. That's why so many Gypsies were driven to steal—so they could buy something to eat. To meet fundamental needs, they continuously migrated, looking for a better place to live. One thing my people didn't understand was that education was the key to success; however, we didn't have the luxury of time nor the ability to defer our hunger that long. We were stuck in this cycle because only by seeking to educate our offspring would we be able to prosper. One thing I am learning at my school in Bucharest is how the world works. I now realize the importance of technology and the reason why some countries prosper and others are left behind. Dimitru is a true friend, and I have discussed my problem with him and told him part of my plan. I need a partner in this. I know that alone and without financial support, I cannot carry out my plan. Yet, there is a part of the plan I cannot divulge. It is a desperate but necessary measure to change six lives profoundly!*

CHAPTER 6

THE INITIAL PLAN

This is my initial plan. I know it is immoral. I think I'm going to improve the lives of all my family. I'm not going to use conventional methods; to accomplish extreme change, I need extreme action. Fundamental to this process will be employing all our skills, talents, and advantages in the most useful way. I'm going to have my sisters learn to speak English since that seems to be the language of the world. In addition I'll make sure they get educated in western culture and manners. Their physical attractiveness is already uncanny. I'm going to teach them all I learned, and my friend is going to help. Dimitru is extremely intelligent and has unlimited financial access.

My plan is as follows: First, my sisters have to adapt to the western style of living and dressing. Loana, who I think might have the best linguistic ability, should learn some Chinese. This will help because my plans for her are to eventually move her to China, specifically Hong Kong. That is where the Western culture mixes with the Eastern, and that city is full of billionaires. All three girls will initially move to London together. There, in London, I need to find a tutor or finishing school to teach them how to act and function among the rich and educated. Mihaela, the oldest and most ambitious of my sisters, needs to learn something that will make getting a job in a five-star hotel easy. As for Daniela, I think I'm going to have her stay in London and learn something about finances. She was very good in mathematics in school and was interested in the challenges of solving problems. With mathematical skills, she might be able to obtain a job in a private wealth-management firm. That would give her access to wealthy men. Once I have my sisters trained, I will need to get them prepared for the second phase. Phase two is how to meet extremely rich men and learn the art of conquering them. A major problem will be how to avoid average men. The real idea is to select highly successful men and use them in a cleaver and disarming way. This is not easily learned; it is manipulation. This is a very delicate subject since I have not told Dimitru the true end game of the plan. My sisters can speak to Dimitru and gain from his personal experience. He has been out in the world in a way they have not been. I am comfortable that I can trust him with my sisters. They can only go out and accept invitations from very wealthy men. I do not want to create a mistress situation, for there is no future in that. I also need to protect them from being drawn into a life of prostitution. All my sisters are very sexy and desirable. My father is having a very difficult time keeping them from getting involved with the boys in our town. The young men are continuously after them. It's very difficult to explain to them the need to avoid dating locally. Gypsies have a reputation of being very sexually active. After we have everything set up, my sisters will need to entice these superwealthy men to fall in love with and marry them.

CHAPTER 7

THE SCHOOL OF HARD KNOCKS

The evening before my trip home, Dimitru went to a soccer match. I did not feel like going, so I took a walk along Victoriei Street and went into a café. That street was loaded with coffee shops and diverse restaurants along with exclusive hotels. After Romania became a democracy, the country changed. Many Romanians that had fled due to the previous Communist regime had returned with money. They came with new ideas, and businesses flourished. Now, Romania had become part of a new Europe. Things were changing so fast that I was worried about how Brexit, Britain's leaving the European Union, would affect my future plan.

By chance, I saw Erik, one of the students from my institute at the coffee shop, and he came over to chat. He was not my type of person, and I would have rather sat alone, but I did not want to be rude. He started to tell me of a place where there was a really good poker game. He had just picked up €5,000 in a few minutes. He began with €20 and was now rich. Erik took out the batch of bills and showed me that it was true.

I wondered how the school had accepted him since he was a very poor student. No one liked to hang out with him. He was planning a trip to London with all that money. His plan was to invite one of the girls that seemed free and easy. This information made me think about getting into the game, where I could try out my luck. I have the thirty thousand euros, so I could take a chance. Not being worldly, I thought, I can take a risk with some of it, and maybe become rich myself.

Erik took me to an old, decrepit building a few blocks away. We went into an apartment, following a complete body search by a monster of a man. We sat down, and at first we only observed how they dealt the cards and how they bet. The dealer was a sleepy-looking old lady who knew how to handle, mix, and deal cards with a straight face. She looked like an immobile robot. After several games, one of the players left, and I took his place. In the next five deals, I won every hand. By then I had accumulated at least four hundred euros. On the sixth deal, after I saw my hand, I felt secure and bet all of it. Since there was no limit, I felt others would drop out since so much money was in the pot. I had three aces, and I felt like a sure winner. Never did I suspect one of the players had a royal flush. I lost, and I was devastated. The big winner gave the dealer a look, and I saw money pass between them.

Now it was more than obvious to me that it was a fixed deck. So, I started to complain, and behind me a bouncer appeared from nowhere. I was lifted out of the chair and took some blows to the head as I was being thrown out onto the street. I left the place bleeding and in pain, and Erik was nowhere to be seen. I learned an expensive and painful lesson.

When I got back to Dimitru's home, I went into the bathroom to tend to my wounds. I evidently left a trail of blood on the floor. A few minutes later Dimitru came in and could not believe what they had done to me. He encouraged me tell him the whole story, which I did. He got on the phone and called three of his father's security guards. Then he insisted on both of us returning to the building where the poker game took place. We arrived at the dilapidated building, and he went in first. Upon entering he was frisked by the beast at the door. Then one by one his security men went in also. Dimitru found Erik having a toast with the owners of the place. They both seemed to be very drunk. A few people were still playing poker and other games.

When Dimitru approached, Erik got up and started explaining that it was not his fault. One of the guards immediately jumped on Dimitru, but he was not fast enough. Dimitru, a karate and judo black belt, instantly knocked him out. The three security men took care of the other gambling employees, who had guns ready to defend their boss. When the outside "monster" heard the altercation, he came in. I was right behind him and I had recuperated enough to trip him and follow it with a crashing blow to the head. It was hard to knock him out. I grabbed the four hundred euros that had been taken from me and left the place in shambles. As we exited the building we found that we were surrounded by police cars, and we were taken to the local police station for questioning. We spent the night at the station. As soon as Dimitru called his father's lawyer, we were released with no charges against us. Dimitru's father had great political strength in Bucharest. This was a day to remember, I had learned many lessons through this painful experience.

CHAPTER 8

CAN BEAUTY BE SHOCKING

Since there was a weekend that extended the New Year's celebration, they had a few days extra away from classes. Dimitru decided to take one of his larger cars on the visit to Constantin's town of Bistriţa. They arrived after a grueling trip, since most roads in Romania are old and in need of repair, taking longer than they thought it would. Google maps were not accurate in this area. They both checked into Hotel Corona de Aur on Plata Petru Rares Street. Constantin asked Dimitru to stay at the hotel so that I could bring his family to meet him. Constantin couldn't call them since they had no phone. They had not entered the twenty-first century yet. The family was expecting him since he had written to his father that he would arrive that day. In the letter he told them to put on their best clothes. He also informed them that he would pick them up in a borrowed car. Recently, Constantin had obtained a driver's license through Dimitru's influence. Borrowing Dimitru's car, he went to his father's shop on the outskirts of town. There they were, and after preliminary hugs and kisses and some tears from mother, they settled down in the car. Constantin started to explain everything as fast as he could while he drove to the hotel.

His mother and father had aged in these past several months, and it was evident. In contrast, his sisters were in the best shape he had ever seen them in. All of them were really gorgeous! He told them about Dimitru and all he had done for him. He spoke about the Agnellis and the plans for the future. They were bewildered by his conversation, and they were not sure what to expect next! Upon arrival, at the hotel they called Dimitru to come down from his room.

When he came down, he could not believe what he saw: three *Playboy*-like models with a beauty beyond expectation. Constantin had not exaggerated his description. Dimitru greeted Constantin's parents and hugged the girls in the Romanian tradition of a hug and a kiss to both cheeks.

CHAPTER 9

HOW DO YOU KNOW WHO TO TRUST

After the preliminary introduction, Matei, Constantin's father, started asking Dimitru questions about his family and his plans. He thanked him with real emotion for all his help and now his incredible offer to help his three daughters. Dimitru noticed that the family dressed in out-of-style clothing and the obvious hardship the family was enduring. He felt the hope they portrayed in their expressions. *Now Dimitru had found a meaningful cause for his life, rather than being just the son of a rich man. In meeting the Wood family and seeing their plight he felt compelled to help. This experience was transformative for Dimitru causing him to realize that his life advantage could be shared and he could rescue an entire family from a hopeless life.*

Dimitru invited the family to sit down in the hotel restaurant, where Constantin whispered in his ear. "Dimitru, my family has never been to a restaurant and are not familiar with anything having to do with etiquette. Let me order for them, and please avoid observing them directly. I'm sure they are very nervous and don't know what to expect in a restaurant."

"Don't worry, my friend, I understand."

The meal went well. Constantin ordered the same dish for everyone. He tried to have a short and relatable conversation. After the meal, Constantin decided to take the family back home because it was getting late. When Matei was alone with Constantin, he explained that the family needed to talk in private with him. They needed to understand the plan going forward. It had only been explained briefly in the car on the way to the hotel.

Matei had lived a long and difficult life and learned a lot of hard lessons about people. He did not know how to tell his son that he was suspicious and uncertain. Constantin's plan felt like a fantasy made up in a book. He told him he couldn't understand how someone could become such close friends with his son, let alone help his son pay for his education and even invest money and time to help him with his three sisters. All this was too much, very difficult to believe. In the car, Constantin's mother, who was usually quiet, had a similar opinion. "How can we trust a stranger and one who isn't a Gypsy?"

Constantin answered with understanding, telling them that he would spend the night at home and explain everything to them.

Daniela commented, "Your friend Dimitru is so handsome, and I noticed he couldn't take his eyes off me! Are you sure he is not after one of us for other reasons?"

The phone rang at the hotel, and it was Constantin calling Dimitru.

"Hi, Dimitru, this is the first time I have seen my family in a long time. I need to spend the evening and night here with them just to catch up. We will get together tomorrow morning, if that is OK with you."

Dimitru, though not happy, understood and quickly responded, "Sure, I understand, and I'll see you tomorrow."

CHAPTER 10

TRUST IS A COMPLICATED MATTER

Upon coming home, Constantin was quickly reminded of the ever present danger of his past life. Even the simple act of parking the car was a major event. It had to be parked in the old stable and the door locked so the car would be safe overnight. Now it was his dad's response that he was looking for. It had been a long time since they were face to face. Time was short so both knew that they had to delve in headlong.

"How did you meet this man? Aren't you afraid that he wants something in payment? How can someone take you into his home? Did he also give you money to buy the clothes you are wearing? How can his parents let a stranger in their home, especially a Gypsy? We have a bad reputation in Bucharest and all over Europe. I hope you are not involved in hashish or opium or other things like that. Please explain!

I trust you, Constantin; you are a good boy and now a man. You promised me that you would do what I haven't been able to accomplish, to take us out of poverty. Honestly, no stealing, nothing illegal." The barrage of questions was something that Constantin expected, but he was tired and not fully ready for them. But who could blame Matei? These were reasonable inquiries. The questions hung in the air. Who could believe in such a philanthropist? Why?

Then Sophy, his mother, who had become very nervous, added, "I have heard that some rich men will do anything to buy a sexual partner. I hope you are not selling your body to that man! All this feels strange to me. I don't want you to go back to Bucharest. You stay here and get yourself a Gypsy woman to love and not a man!"

The intensity of everyone was clear. Constantin had no time to answer even the first question before everyone was on him with more of their concerns. Daniela immediately said, "Mother, Constantin is a straight man. I know he had dated a few girls in my school, and they all say he is macho. The way his friend looked at me, Dimitru is definitely not a homosexual."

"I'm sure he is not," Mihaela laughingly said. "I can't believe what my mother thinks! Constantin gay? No way!"

Slowly Constantin responded, "I don't blame any of you for your concern. Let me try to answer some of your questions and try to quiet some of your fears. I can see that in my absence everyone's imagination is running wild. Dimitru is really a nice and intelligent man. I have been lucky, as he met me in a difficult moment in his life and felt that I was the person he could talk to. I instantly liked him as well. We both had a need. I guess that I became a project for him when he saw I was in need of everything that he had plenty of: money, connections, and social status. Though I started as a project, we began to share confidences and rely on one another. He seems to need something from me. I'm not sure, but he does seem to appreciate our close friendship and my advice and honest perspective. I am at a difficult and confusing moment in my life and this caused us both to talk to and trust each other."

Loana asked, "What problem does he have?"

"Well, he is an only child, and his parents were always traveling, building their business. He was brought up by different nannies. His mother is insecure and kept on firing the sweet, caring nannies who were very good and gentle to him. She feared he would not give her his love due to competition with the nannies. He and his mother are not close, and his father is always busy with business. Now it seems his parents realize this and hope to keep him at home to create an adult bond with them. The price of wealth was their son's closeness. There was no time to talk and hang out with him. So when Dimitru met me, he liked me. During our talks I described my problems and my plans and objectives. Since he felt I was in dire need, he felt I could be trusted. As I shared he become excited and wants to make my objectives his. I need to share with you as well that he is my match in mathematics. I am astounded by his ability, and his overall intelligence is amazing.

He is terrific at strategy as well. I helped him cope with his family, and he will help me with mine. His father gave him the freedom of spending on anything he wanted. Since he reversed his decision to pursue school in the US, both parents were happy that he finally found a friend. Now they could travel without the worry of him staying alone. This might be difficult for you to understand, but it happened, and this young man is a true friend. I'm sure he is like a brother, and he told me to let you know that he will treat you like sisters. Don't fear; he will not try to have an affair with any of you."

Sadly, Daniela asked if he had a relationship at the moment. Constantin told her no, with a worried look on his face.

Every member of the Woods family were moved by the enthusiasm that Constantin exuded about the future underwritten by Dumitru and his family. The mixed emotions stirred in each, in their own unique way.

CHAPTER 11

LOANA'S DIARY

As Constantin left the house, Loana drifted into her own thoughts, memories, and concerns. She decided that this was the beginning of her adult life and she would now keep a diary. She would reflect on her past and record events as they happened.

Our home is Bistriţa. It is the capital city of Bistriţa-Nasaud County. We are in Northern Transylvania-Romania, and we are situated on the Bistriţa River. Our river has a big dam and a lake. My city has a population of one hundred thirty thousand and administers to six villages. Our village is Sarata. Once we were a part of Hungary, and during a time were under German administration. We live in a Gypsy commune called Zagra, near the Carpathian Mountains. My father, Matei, was the type who didn't want us to mingle with the rest of the neighborhood. Therefore, our house was on the upper part of a hill. My father always tried to stop us from becoming part of all the immorality that occurred in the Gypsy neighborhood.

Sexually the neighbors were loose, and my father's and mother's values were different. During weekends we didn't leave the house. Drunken men waited on the hidden parts of the hills for a girl. No matter what her age, they would attempt to molest or rape her. My neighborhood is that way, and that's what my father always warned us about. Surprisingly, Bistriţa has several schools, and my father never let us go to school alone. He always took us and picked us up. He was a very big and muscular man who always carried a defensive weapon. The locals knew us, and no one dared to approach him to fight or steal from us. They knew they had no chance. One day when I was fourteen, three guys tried to jump him and abduct the three of us. They were badly hurt, and his reputation in the area became well known. The message to all was not to mess with Matei or his son, Constantin. His shop was not far from our neighborhood, and most of the customers were from other villages. A shop like his was a meeting point since he traded items like a pawn shop and also sold tobacco.

Now that we are out of school, we have even less contact with local friends. We take a nearby bus to the public library in downtown Bistriţa. This library frequently has English courses. Sometimes they invite foreigners to teach another language. That's how I started learning Mandarin, which is not an easy language. When it comes to English, I'm really good. I am better than my sister Daniela, but Mihaela is a language genius. What a surprise. When we began, no one knew that she had this gift. She hears it, and she remembers it. That made her a natural for languages. We were all shocked when suddenly she began reading the paperwork that came with the cigarettes and other smokes in Dad's store. She read the foreign languages, and she could tell us what it meant. At first Dad thought she was kidding and making this up. Later on when he checked with the man who sells him the products, he found that she was accurate with her translation. The packs were from all over, and many of them she could translate.

Now Mrs. Mullen at the library knows all of us very well. Since we all finished school, we have nothing to do, so we practically live in the library. Mrs. Mullen asked Mihaela to teach some of the languages she is good at. She even offered to pay my father. Even though the money would have helped a lot, he did not want that to interfere with him picking us up after he closed his shop. Nights were not safe for us.

I asked my mother why they called me Loana, and she said that had been the name of my father's grandmother, and it means "light." My parents say they love me and take care of me more now than ever. My parents say they love and care for me more than the others, as I am youngest and most intelligent, but that's not true; they love us all. We spend almost all day in the library—that's what our father insists on, and my mother goes along with him. My father's intention is for us to have a better life than our parents have had. In the library we have gotten to explore magazines that reflect what is going on in the outside world. We have seen photos of places we didn't even know existed. Now that the library has brought in computers, the world has really opened up to us. Dad was right; it is important to learn, and the English we have picked up has helped us greatly on the computer. We also go to every talk on all subjects—politics, news, music, and art—that happen several times a week in the library. Sometimes there is free food, especially when an important person comes from Bucharest. Those are our favorite days. All the employees know us, and we lend a hand when the library is busy. Daniela helps the woman who replaces the books on the shelves, and she is an expert in doing that.

Our library is in the Piata Centrala area, right near the Saxon Evangelical Church. On Sundays we go to that church because they give everyone a free meal. But we always take apples and bread along with whatever my father finds so we do not get hungry. My opinion is that we are not fat like other girls because we eat very little. I think we do not have to go to the doctor because we don't eat food that has empty calories. We eat a lot of fruit and vegetables every day. My father is not like other men; he doesn't drink or smoke, even though he sells tobacco products. He has taught us that tobacco kills people. His advice comes from his experience. We do not have grandparents because all his family died from too much drinking, unhealthy eating, and smoking. As a family we get along and don't fight.

My mother doesn't ever talk about her past or her family. We can't even guess what happened. My father has told us that his family live in a city near the Black Sea, the city of Constanta. We are quite curious and want to go there, but we do not have money for that, and truthfully we don't want to uncover what should be hidden. All our family money was put away for Constantin's technology education in Bucharest.

Last year the library started to teach computer and tech-nology since now they have Wi-Fi and Internet. Bucharest sent twenty new computers and some printers. As soon as we finished school, Constantin and my father insisted we need to study and learn about everything. In the near future, we will be going to London and America, but I have always been interested in China. Because of my interest, I have studied some Chinese. The library has two hundred CDs, and believe it or not, that's what I listen to almost every day. I have one person I practice with when she comes on Fridays, and she is a native speaker. My brother's plan for us is something that we talk about often but alone; it's our only hope. Finally, our lives are beginning to change, but can we handle a foreign country, alone? None of us have ever been alone, not even for one day.

Dear Diary there is more to come soon, the future is right in front of me.

CHAPTER 12

SOPHY'S SECRETS

As Constantin returned to Bucharest and the plan was laid out for the family, his mother, Sophy, prepared for major life changes. She had been down this road before as a young woman herself.

I have been extremely nervous since my son, Constantin, came back from Bucharest. He brought this friend from the Institute where he studies, and since then I have even been more anxious. Matei, my husband, is so strict in his ideas, he won't let my girls go to parties or anywhere alone. He is afraid they might become pregnant, or runaway, like many young girls do. I know from my own personal experience. I was born in Hungry and it was in Communist hands. All my family became Communists since it was the only way to survive. They became thieves and stole from the wealthy and did horrible things. In 1989 it became a free country, and Janos Kadar, the horrible Communist dictator, was deposed. However, my family never changed. The way that I met Matei was one night when I was out hunting for food for the family I was hungry and desperate and ready to do anything. Instead of taking me to the bar for a quick sexual act, he fell in love with me and that same night took me to Romania. He was so good to me; he never hit me like the other men do to their wives. He cared for me and worried about me. I immediately got pregnant with Constantin, and then I had three beautiful girls, one after the other. Mihaela is twenty, Daniela nineteen, and Loana eighteen. My Constantin is twenty-one, tall, and very handsome, like his father. I don't talk about my family. From what I hear they have not changed. They still do illegal things: They falsify documents, trade in illegal drugs, and might be involved in kidnappings. They are still Communists and think that everything belongs to them. My children don't know them, and I have always been afraid that my birth family would kill me if they knew that Matei was a Gypsy. They hate Gypsies, and they used to say they had killed many. I'm in constant fear of them finding me. I changed my name, but it's been twenty-one years of fear. I know Constantin always hints about knowing my past, and I hope Matei doesn't tell him the truth. Currently we are so poor and needy, yet Matei wants too look only for billionaires for our daughters. Constantin's plan is too difficult. I feel it's impossible. I don't trust that friend; I don't trust any friend. All my life has been difficult. My family, who I don't talk about, destroyed me when I was young. We had no values, I want a better life for my children!

CHAPTER 13

DANIELA'S ANTICIPATION

Drifting off into her thoughts, as were the other members of the family, Daniela mused; *I'm, nineteen, the shortest in the family, yet I am great at sports. However, I'm a prisoner in my own home. I'm limited to whatever I can do in my small home and backyard. I have a basketball ring on a wall, and my father brought me a basketball from the shop. Now I'm really good at shooting at the basket, as well as at playing Ping-Pong. When I was in school, I was the best goalie in soccer. Even the boys team wanted me to play with them. I haven't seen any of my friends in two years. I had to keep the boys away from me. They drive me crazy, but my parents won't let us do anything outside of their company. It's really my father, he doesn't understand young girls and our needs. All this loneliness and isolation have made me very anxious.*

Since I have no friends to talk to, I have developed this habit where I can't stop pulling at my hair until it falls out. I wear a ponytail so no one can tell. Everyone in the family is constantly saying, "Daniela, stop!" but I feel better, so I continue to do it. I have big breasts, and the boys always try to peek at my cleavage. However, my clothes don't expose my figure. We are not allowed to wear revealing clothes, but that's another story. My English is pretty good. I need to learn some more phrases and idioms. The good news is Constantin's connections will move me forward and to another country. Then I will not have my parents' eyes watching me. My brother's plan is for me to work in a famous hotel. I wonder what kind of a job I could do in a hotel? I have never even been in the rooms of a hotel. My only experience of a hotel was in the dining room when we met Dimitru, Constantin's friend. That is when his best friend looked at me with obvious attraction. I found him to be very handsome. I'll see what happens. I feel he likes me, and I felt good about it.

CHAPTER 14

LIFE IS PASSING ME BY

Silently absorbed with her own frustration Mihaela. thought; *at twenty years old, I have no husband, no chil-dren, and no friends outside the immediate family. I am ready for my life to begin, and today Constantin presented the plan for my future. I am very excited and frightened at the same time. It has not been easy living in this horrible neighborhood. My father doesn't let my sisters and me dress like women. We have no pants, only long skirts and long-sleeve shirts, all worn out and mended many times. He doesn't let us mingle with the other young people, and we can't ever go to dances or parties. When I was in school, years ago, all the girls I knew had some type of sexual experience. We three only talk about what the girls told us. Life is passing me by. My father is a tyrant, even though I love him. I'm sure he means well. Several boys stare at me, they are handsome but I don't dare respond to them. My father and brother have a great plan for a great future for me. I'm hoping to go to America. Everyone wishes to go to*

America, and I will! I'm lucky to have had a hobby, and that's what will probably help me obtain my freedom. My future will be guaranteed, as I'm great at languages. I have learned using books and CDs how to speak, English, Swahili, Farsi, and some Arabic. I can't write Arabic very well, but I can understand and express my thoughts. I wanted to study Chinese, but since my sister Loana started to learn that, I did not want to compete with her. I let her have all the books and CDs that we were able to borrow at the main library.

Trying to be objective, I know that I am an attractive young woman. That part of myself has not yet been seen by the outside world. At the library we have used the computers, and I have seen all kinds of photos of beautiful women. It's amazing, but we three are all in that category. With the proper makeup and clothing, we could be models. Maybe that is what Constantin has in mind for us? I don't care if it is my ability in language or my looks; it's time for life to begin! We have good parents, and they have protected us until now. Since we are young, they feed us first, and if there is something leftover, then they eat. They want us to be ladies and learn from books how the educated and rich live. My father brings home all the old magazines that people bring to sell from his shop. I believe that in the US they call his kind of store a pawn shop. His shop is very small, and he barely makes money for food for us. Now is the time for me to take a bite out of life and enjoy the risks that come with that!

CHAPTER 15

DIMITRU'S ROCK BOTTOM

Back in town Dumitru was alone for the night and deep
in thought.

*Well, here I am in a strange town with the evening and
night to myself. I think I will take a short walk and explore the
town. This is where Constantin grew up; it seems to be very
limited. I have only walked a few blocks, and I'm at the edge
of town. I may as well go back and have dinner at the hotel
restaurant. The menu was interesting and had some dishes with
which I was not familiar.*

Then came a decisive moment: "Sir, what beverage would
you like with dinner? We have a full bar."

Dimitru was confronted in that moment with a flood of
feelings and thoughts. His first thought was yes, but then his
promise to his parents came back to him. He recalled the
bouts of drinking that had left him with lost time periods
in his life. Their words were ringing in his ears when he said,
"Yes, thank you, I'll have a double Johnny Walker Black on

the rocks." *It's one drink; what's the big deal? I guess I'll have a quiet evening and an early night.*

The bar was almost empty, and then a couple came in and sat in a booth close to him. After a few minutes, they started arguing, and the shouting was really out of place. Dumitru was feeling very relaxed, and when the waiter asked, he automatically said yes to a second and then a third drink. Now he was really at ease, more comfortable than he had been in a long time. He had missed this feeling. He seemed to be much more at ease when his friend Constantin was nearby. Dumitru never thought that anything would bring him a secure feeling like the new deep friendship had brought. Constantin was a very special guy.

Suddenly, the man in the next booth slapped the woman. Dumitru got up to stop this, even though he was a little wobbly. The guy landed an unexpected solid hit to Dimitru's head. He fell to the floor, and stayed there for a moment, even though he was feeling no pain—the drinks had done their job. Then he got up and in one minute knocked this stranger to the floor. Dimitru's training had worked even though he was not 100 percent. Dimitru's automatic response was to overpower him by leverage and subdue him. The stranger asked for pity and not continue, that his pain was excruciating.

"I will release you, but if I ever hear that you hit a defenseless woman again, I will find you, and we will continue this." The guy flew out of the hotel, leaving the frightened girl crying. By now the hotel security and other personnel were in the bar. They thanked Dumitru for getting rid of the abuser, who always came with a different woman. It seemed that he found it erotic to beat them in public. Dimitru sat next to the lady and asked her if she was OK. She thanked him and asked for a drink. She admitted that didn't know this man prior to meeting this afternoon. She felt that accepting the date in a public place seemed safe. The current conversation was facilitated by two more drinks. By now Dumitru was drunk, and she was slurring her words. He knew this was dangerous for him because of past experiences. Now he had broken his promise to his parents.

The girl said she needed to get home, and the public bus to her town had stopped running at eleven o'clock. She did not have a place to spend the night. Dimitru asked the hotel clerk if he could get a taxi for her, but no service was found. So he told her she could stay in his room since his friend was not staying that night. She hesitated, but Dimitru had seemed so kind and interested in helping her go home that she felt a level of trust. What she did not know was that Dimitru was very dizzy. He went up to his room with difficulty, and she followed. That night was a night to remember, but he was so drunk that he didn't remember what happened. When he got up the next morning, the girl was naked and on top of him. Constantin walked into the room, saw what was going on, and closed the door. Both Constantin and Dimitru were hard pressed by these circumstances. Each had a lot to think about, consider, and discuss, but not now. Now they had to scramble and make things right.

Constantin had been up most of the night, talking with his family. As the two friends had agreed, he returned to the hotel room at nine o'clock the next morning. Once there he found Dimitru in this compromising situation. Quickly, Dimitru regained his composure. He told the girl to dress and get out. He too had had an intense night. What led him to having sex with her? He knew he was drunk and that she was right next to him. Then he remembered that in the early morning, she had started to touch him and whispered that she was turned on and offered to have oral sex with him. He was too tired and groggy, and he refused. She insisted by fondling and touching him and exciting him. As she proceeded, he noticed that she had taken out a small vial, and she brought it up to her mouth. He stopped her and pinned her to the bed, and asked what the hell she was doing. Then with fear of being hurt, she told him the plot. She told him that whenever she had a chance of getting a wealthy man in bed, she tried to preserve the semen. Then she sold it to a man she knew. He would wait in the hotel and use nitrogen to freeze and preserve the sample. Then it was sold to customers who wanted to have children that have wealthy and strong genes. She also mentioned something about DNA content to be used for blackmailers.

"So how did you choose me?"

After prodding and insisting, she told him that the man who brought her to the hotel had been informed that he was in the hotel and that he was rich. "He called me to do my job on you." Dimitru was totally awake by now, and furious about what had happened. He should have never touched the whisky. After hearing this story, he grabbed the willing girl and had rough sex with her, and just as it was ending, Constantin had opened the door.

CHAPTER 16

HONESTY IS THE NAME OF THE GAME

Constantin walked back to his room when he saw the girl leave the hotel. A man was waiting for her, and she looked very anxious. Dimitru went ahead and told him everything that had happened in the last few hours. He admitted his drinking problem and asked his best friend to help him when he strayed. Constantin shared everything he had experienced at home, all the questions and comments made by everyone that night. After he mentioned the Daniela comment, Dimitru smiled.

"I see she has detected my interest in her. Sorry, Constantin. You have such hot sisters, and that Daniela goes above and beyond my dreams of the ideal woman."

"Dimitru, remember your promise to treat them as sisters, please. My friend, I can see that you have some issues of your own that have been demons and that you need to conquer. Your interest in Daniela can abort all our plans. My parents are very observant and are afraid of your intentions. You can't blame them for not trusting you. Our family has always been taken advantage by local people, and everyone. We are distrustful people."

Dimitru then got a phone call from his father asking his whereabouts and asking him to return as soon as possible. His father needed his help with something delicate that had come up that very morning. Dimitru made some phone calls and had Constantin drive him to the local airport. There he rented a Cessna and left for Bucharest. He gave Constantin his car to use to return to Bucharest.

CHAPTER 17

LIKE SON, LIKE FATHER

Mr. Agnelli Sr. was very successful; he had been weathered by life. Physically he was a tall, handsome, and determined man. He had just received a call from a secretary that had worked for him in one of his many offices. This call shook him to the core because she told him she was pregnant with his child and that she could prove it.

"I didn't believe her, so I hung up. Not ten minutes later, that fellow Erick, who studies at your school, sent me an e-mail. He threatened to make this public unless you meet with him. Look, son, I want to explain. I went to a long and boring conference, where I had a few too many drinks. It caused me to wind up in bed with this young woman. It's all a blur, and it was not intentional. I only have a very fuzzy memory of this happening. This is one of the reasons that I have encouraged you to stop drinking, as I have stopped now, after this event. All I can recall is, that evening after the conference and after several drinks, this young woman started rubbing herself on me. She was being seductive, and I was flattered. Me, an old man, being approached by this girl. We danced together, and she was all over me. She whispered that she wanted to be alone with me for five minutes. Since my head was not in the right place, I took her to my car. In the back seat, we had intercourse, which ended in two minutes. I didn't even think about safety, nor did I have a condom. I was a victim of my indiscrete drinking. Your mother can't find out about this! That's imperative! I leave this in your hands. It is my turn to need your help. Please don't judge me, I have stopped drinking, and I realize how vulnerable I am when I am drunk."

Dimitru remembered that Erick's sister had worked for his father's company. He knew that he had to act fast and resolve this situation. Dimitru was aware of Erick's lack of character and wondered what kind of scam this was.

CHAPTER 18

THE PLAN IS INITIATED

When he was home again, Constantin gathered with his three sisters. His father and mother were in their shop, trying to buy and sell whatever they came by. Constantin explained to his sisters that they should continue be studying English in the library were they were well known. They were amazed because he reached into his pocket and gave them a lot of money for that purpose. Next, he gave them a list of books and magazines to buy, one about etiquette and others about different types of possible professions. He explained that they needed to work hard and quickly become worldlier. In addition they had to join the twenty-first century. In order to do, so they needed to learn to research using a computer. He told them to buy a used one somewhere. For each task he handed them a fistful of money.

They could not believe their eyes. How did Constantin get so much money, where did it come from, and what did he owe for this? All three had questions, but right now they were just listening and processing what he was telling them. This was to be their future. It was really going to happen; he had the money to make it real. He wanted Mihaela, who had a very nice voice, to practice American songs. He wanted Loana to study Chinese culture and habits and some words and sayings in Mandarin. As for Daniela, she was taking medicine because she had been diagnosed with having panic attacks in the past. He asked her to take it a little slower than the others. She needed to keep a paper bag with her in case she had a panic incident. He reminded her not to stop her medicine, and he gave her another box of pills he'd brought from Bucharest. He informed his sisters that they had three months to get ready. In three months he would obtain passports to travel to London to start their life changing plan. He warned all three to keep this a total secret. He hinted that any information getting out could ruin the family's plan for dramatic change. He promised that their parents would be well and that he would be able to help them with Dimitru's support. Then he reminded Daniela and the other two that they were close to escaping the Gypsy cycle of life. They needed to keep away from the guys that were always after their affection. Around three o'clock in the afternoon, he received a call from Dimitru asking him to please drive back to Bucharest immediately. He had a personal problem to resolve, and he needed Constantin's help. Constantin did not hesitate one moment. He drove to say good-bye to his parents and left them the money they may need.

CHAPTER 19

CLOSE CALL AVERTED

C onstantin had an opportunity to help and repay part of the family debt to Dimitru's father. Constantin was to secretly find and meet Erick's sister. She was twenty-one and didn't know him. Being a young attractive man, he was to flirt with her and seduce her while plying her with liquor. Then he was going to find out if she was actually pregnant. He would suggest a condom for fear of pregnancy and gauge her response. He would wait to hear "It's not necessary; I'm already pregnant." That would expose if this was, or was not a scam to extort money from Dimitri's father. On the other side of the equation, Dimitru was going to meet with Erick and feel out his demands while working his way into Erick's confidence. Dimitru knew that he could do that by offering him a high-paying job with his father's company. This approach was to start immediately.

Constantin was directed to the office in town that she was supposed to be working in. He didn't know her, but after a brief flirt with the receptionist, he was able to find out which desk was hers. Now that he had located her, he needed to create a chance meeting. He waited, and at dinner time he followed her to a nearby coffee shop and sat in the booth behind her. She was on her cell phone talking to someone about a movie she wanted to see. The conversation ended soon, and she made another call, trying to convince a girl named Carol to go to the movies with her. She seemed frustrated since this was her second turndown. After she hung up, Constantin saw this as an opening and realized he could use this pretext rather than liquor.

He picked up his cell phone and acted out a phone call to someone asking him to go to that same movie she had spoken about, playing off that he had received a rejection also. He did this in a stage whisper, and it was loud enough for her to hear. The waitress came over, and even though she was a woman of about sixty, Constantin jokingly asked her to leave work and go to the movie with him.

She responded, "I'd love to, but I have to work, dear."

He looked at the next booth, his target, and said, "No one wants to go to the movies with me."

He immediately heard the response, "I'd love to go!"

Then he knew he was on track to get the information needed for Mr. Agnelli Sr. Step one was completed. He invited her to sit in his booth, and as she looked at him, a smile come across her face, and she lit up. That smile was not about the movie.

She said, "How unbelievable! I'm also looking for someone to go to the same movie. What's your name?"

He told her he was Karl, just in case she mentioned it to her brother. Then she said her name was Ann. The time was getting tight, so they went straight to the movie. She was impressed with the car he drove, a Lexus, which is rare in Romania. They carried on some small talk, and Constantin looked for a swollen belly. She might have had this sign since four months had elapsed since her encounter with Dimitru's father. I saw no enlargement since her belly was very slim.

The movie was not his type, full of love scenes, but it did get her in the right frame of mind, and she grabbed his knee when it was almost finished. She asked if he was gay since he had not made a move on her yet. The answer was a kiss and a strong hug. Ann asked if he wanted to go to a dance hall she knew of. That might have been dangerous because his classmates hung out there, and Erik could've even been there. He said no and stopped to pick up two sandwiches, and they started to make out. He attempted to touch her sexually, with no resistance. When she was obviously excited, he asked her when her last period was, and she said it was seven days ago and that she was on the pill and they didn't need to worry about a condom. That was it; that's all he needed to know. He proceeded to complain about a severe muscle pain in his leg and told her he could drop her off at home and would see her the next day. She was not too happy since she was excited, but she understood his pain. Constantin then called Dimitru and gave him the good news. He had been sitting in a bar with Erik, who he told he would call soon with a job in one of their refineries overseas. He was promised a high salary, which was Erick's attempted extortion. Dimitru never even had to address the pregnancy blackmail. Dimitru informed his father that they had accomplished the mission and that the blackmail was without merit.

CHAPTER 20

A WALK ON THE DARK SIDE

"**W**e don't want my sisters to be traced to my hometown, to my family's extreme poverty, and to the fact of our ethnic origin."

Dimitru was distracted and deep in thought, and he did not dispute this fact, nor did he question it.

"It's also necessary to change their names and birthdays.

Dimitru suggested that the first thing we should do is get them authentic documents so that if they ever got into an identity problem they could take out their real information. Constantin was amazed by Dimitru's worldliness, as he was familiar with a forger. He shared that he used him to get a driver's license at fifteen. They followed up on this suggestion and contacted a Turkish man who prepared the perfect driver's license a few years before. We were told that all of his other documents were perfect too.

Dimitru said, "We will give him pictures of your sisters, and he will do a fabulous job."

"Dimitru, how much are you spending on all this?"

He responded, "Don't worry, brother, I'm sure in the future you and I will be successful, and you will repay me. Maybe your sisters will be so well off that they will repay us too, but that is for a future date. Please, Constantin, don't worry about money."

Constantin had his sisters' birth certificates and pictures and handed them to Kfir, the Turk, who transformed people's identities. He was well-known in illegal circles, and he paid the police well to continue to operate. Rumors were that many Iranians and Syrians with money came to get new IDs for their families. They needed these to get visas to some countries that forbade people from their national homelands. He covered all the details, even down to the stamps, and he had legal papers from everywhere; it was impressive to see. His storefront sold Turkish rugs, but they didn't think he sold many rugs, yet he was visited by many people all day long.

At first, when they went and told him what they wanted, he said he was very busy and couldn't accept the order. Dimitru showed him his ID, and Kfir realized who he was, and then he asked them to give him two hours to get the papers ready. When they returned Mihaela was a Brazilian, Daniela was Belgian, and Loana stayed Romanian, but she was born in Chernovitz, a city that now belonged to Ukraine. That made it difficult or impossible to double-check on the veracity of these documents. They were very excited because this was the first concrete step in the implementation of the plan to reach a dream objective: for the Woods family to leave poverty behind forever.

CHAPTER 21

CHANGE BRINGS ANXIETY

Mihaela's tall, five-foot-eleven body eased into the room. She moved quickly and approached Constantin with the smoothness of movement that reflected her athletic ability and experience. As was her habit, she entered the room with a whisper of singing. Her beautiful voice was the only thing that clued Constantin that she was there. In a flash, he glanced at her reflective blond hair. Her hair always made her stand out in the town, and all the young men were enamored with her. It was a curious fact since most Gypsies have dark hair and a darker complexion than other nationalities.

Her face gave off a mysterious and inquisitive sexy look. She had no formal training in foreign languages. She only knew the English she had gathered from the use of the computer in the library. Therefore, she was challenged by the idea of the need to be proficient in English and Portuguese. From her singing she had memorized a few Portuguese songs, but she did not know their meaning. A major part of her brother's blueprint for her was presenting herself as refined and feminine. To accomplish this she was going to have to suppress her athletic self. Could all these challenges be met? As the ideas of the "plan" filled the room, excitement swirled in the air. What other expectations or challenges would there be? How would it be to leave the family? She would be a stranger in a strange land. Who would be there to support her efforts? Her dad was always there at her athletic matches to cheer her on. She needed to learn English and Brazilian customs. Information about life in those countries would be something that she needed to pursue. Since she love music and singing she chose to learn the songs of these languages. Also needed was femininity, which would cause her to give up her favorite sports, wrestling and kickboxing. She would start studying English two hours every day. She used the computer and video tapes to perfect her pronunciation. They had the best collection of English and Portuguese CDs to help her memorize the songs.

At the same time, Loana entered into her diary;, *My sisters are beautiful and smart. What if they succeed and marry wealthy men, and I fail to even learn a language? What if Constantin goes to all this trouble to arrange everything for me, and I give myself away, or what if I am not up to the task? Maybe I should stay here and marry the boy from town. He looks at me every day, and he has not married yet. He hopes that I will give in one day and say yes. I have never lived in any other language, and he wants me to learn two languages—Mandarin and English. In school we never studied language."*

Daniela too was deep in thought. Though she was also very beautiful and had an excellent personality, she was having her doubts. She would need to learn everything about Belgium. Besides learning English she needed to be able to manage French.;*My skill is in being able to dance beautifully, and I am graceful. Now I will begin to study English at the same time as Mihaela and Loana," Daniela thought. "Constantin's friend sounds nice, so maybe I don't have to go through all that Constantin wants me to do. What if I get caught with a foreign passport? Won't they send me to jail? I could not survive there. My anxieties would be much too great. If our goal is to marry rich, maybe I could marry him. I am five foot four, and I have black hair; they tell me that I am beautiful. I see how the boys look at me. Maybe Dimitru will like me enough to marry me. Then I won't have to do all this. Perhaps my beautiful blue eyes and incredible memory could win him over. My memory is wonderful, and I guess that I will begin listening to the CDs that Constantin sent me for language practice so I can have a head start.*

CHAPTER 22

MYSTERY OF THE PAST/UNCERTAINTY OF THE FUTURE

Dimitru returned from seeing his parents off on a trip and asked Constantin to give him an update on "the plan."

"I have been very busy with implementation. My three sisters have begun their training. I sent them one of the old cell phones you gave me, and now we communicate all the time. It seems that they are also facilitating our plan. Loana met a Chinese woman in her English class, and she agreed to teach her the basics of Mandarin. Dimitru, there is something that I have been thinking about for many years. I decided to call my mother, when my father was in his shop, and see if she is willing to talk about her family. I have no idea why she has kept this an area of 'please don't ask.' We are old enough to know her secret. What city did she come from, and who is her family? We have never met them, and we have no contact with them. Their absence is glaring. I thought about it again when I was handling all our ID documents. The line asking for mother's parents' names was left blank on all of them. I am building up to it, and one day soon, I am going to make that call. At this point I am so busy with the future that the past will have to wait.

Today as part of my research for our plan, I called the British consulate. They told me that visas are not required for Brazil or any of the European countries. We won't have a problem with that. The problem will be getting a visa to the US for Mihaela and one for Loana to Hong Kong. I'll worry about that later."

Dimitru said, "Our family is very friendly with the American ambassador here in Bucharest. Maybe he can help with the US visa?"

Constantin speculated, "I don't think he can since my information is that the Consulate is very strict and requires a lot of paperwork. Proof of bank accounts and other requirements are needed. Our plan to use a passport from Brazil, makes it even more complicated."

Dimitru responded, "In case we are not successful, we can get her to Mexico and have her enter like most Mexicans do. Trump's wall isn't up yet."

"OK, let's see what happens. What is your timetable? Dimitru asked, why are we limited to three months?"

Constantin responded, "In three months we finish the program at the Institute. I'll go back and pick up my sisters, and maybe we can take the train to France, then to London via the canal tunnel."

Understanding the time frame Dimitru utilized his organizational talent and assumed the responsibility to use these coming months to arrange a London apartment and all of the elements necessary for the implementation of a new life for these three young woman.

Both now had their charted responsibilities and pieces of the plan to push towards the completion of this life changing task.

CHAPTER 23

RESTLESS THOUGHTS/ MANY QUESTIONS, FEW SOLUTIONS

Constantin had been thinking about the implementation of the plan in the United States for Mihaela. His key to the door of success was to have his sister marry, or become available to acquire evidence of sexual misconduct with a billionaire. Several possibilities went through his mind. Blackmail might have to be their goal. All of the logistics were yet to be determined. Constantin's recent experiences had shown him that seductive woman were able to manipulate rich men using their sexuality and the weapon of guilt and embarrassment. Guilt could be either legal or moral and could lead to untold riches. He still needed to resolve the specific methods to succeed. So many questions: How will we get her into the United States? cact with extremely wealthy men when they are alone?

What techniques would she have to use to collect or acquire their seamen. Would she need to become pregnant. Could she, or would she participate in this plot? If she were pregnant what would constitute proof in a court of law?

Secretly I have double-checked the internet, and in the United States, you go to any chain pharmacy, like Walgreens, and buy a DNA paternity kit. It is less than eighty dollars, and that includes lab fees. The next issue is how to test the man's DNA to prove that it is a match. Mihaela will need to bring a DNA sample from the man. That can be accomplished by taking his toothbrush which will not be noticeable and will seem innocuous. Should it be necessary to go to court it will be handled by a representing lawyer. There may or may not be a need for an actual pregnancy. I will only involve her with a healthy, rich men. There can be no other sentimental attachments. I will investigate and discover where the super wealthy stay when they are in New York City. That will be the hotel, where Mihaela works. More preliminary is the idea that it might be too risky to cross the Mexican border to the US. Though Dimitru expressed this as an option, I will explore another legal way of getting her into the United States. One that comes to mind is to have her accompany a United States citizen as his fiancée. That's more complicated because we need to add a new person to our plan, which I don't think is wise. I need to continue to think about this ...

I hate to think of this because I don't trust Erick. He is a green-card holder, but we have had such bad incidents with him. He is awaiting a call from Mr. Agnelli Sr. to send him to one of the US companies. They had promised him a job in order to get rid of him. We can use him as our fiancée carrier and send him to a mainland US office. This way, she can enter as his fiancée and get a legal visa. It's very risky; but he can be controlled if necessary. After he serves our purpose, I can then get Dimitru to transfer him to the Brazilian office in Sao Paulo or the office in Cape Town, South Africa. He is going to ask many questions, I know, but I will search for a story that will neutralize him. We will him busy with something else. Well, that's a possibility. Dimitru's alternative of going through the Mexican border is too hazardous, and she will just be another illegal with no papers. That would make it impossible to get a job. Being illegal would risk her status with a court to pursue police assistance and legal remedies. I need to rethink the plan so that it works out smoothly and successfully.

So far, in this part of the plan, I am on my own. I am afraid of sharing this information with Dimitru. He does not know the pain of a life of poverty.

For right now I need to focus on our short term goal, and solve the concerns involved with our next immediate steps. London, and training.

CHAPTER 24

BLUEPRINT FOR LONDON

Dimitru called with excitement in his voice, "Constantin, I just spoke to one of my father's associates, Peter French, in London. His mother just retired. She used to teach English and etiquette at a well-known school for girls. She herself is very cultured and wants to keep busy. She might be the perfect person to train your sisters. I explained to Mr. French that a friend who was planning to move to England had three sisters who needed instruction in English and culture in general. That's when he mentioned his mother. Our first step is to find an apartment near her home and have the girls live there while being tutored. He will help me. He has been my father's right-hand man in England for many years. I know that he appreciates all we have done for him. I have met him several times on trips to London with my family.

"There are so many basic details to attend to, Dimitru, we also need my sisters to have a wardrobe, as they have very little to wear."

"Don't worry I'm with you on this; I'm sure that Mrs. French will help them. I will also make sure we get them individual credit cards and IDs, and I will deposit sufficient money in a bank account for them to avoid problems. What are your thoughts about all of this?"

"Dimitru, you are more than a brother; you are an angel, I don't know how I'm going to thank or repay you."

"Dear Constantin, I feel you are like a brother I never had, and this is the family that I have longed for all my life." When we are together I finally feel comfortable

CHAPTER 25

LANGUAGES ARE WORTH THEIR WEIGHT IN GOLD

onstantin met Dimitru after their last class on Friday, and they decided to have a beer together, to celebrate since they had only one more week of school left. Beer was something quite new to Constantin, who was brought up with the warning that alcohol was what killed his paternal grandparents. Matei frequently repeated that "all Gypsies die from alcohol addiction." Dimitru had often had a beer or two when they dined together, but this was the first time Constantin decided to have one also.

Constantin started the conversation, talking about the problem of getting Mihaela into the US legally. He shared that using Erick was very dangerous and could backfire. Dimitru asked if the older sister, Mihaela, had any specific outstanding qualities. Constantin mentioned all the languages she had studied alone in their town's public library.

He stated that she has an excellent memory and spoke several languages.

Dimitru perked up at hearing this and asked which languages she spoke.

As best as he could recall Constantin listed the languages she had studied: Farsi, Arabic, Swahili, and English, and since Romanian come from Latin, she understands some Spanish.

Dimitru realized that he could use this ability to get Mihaela into the United States legally. Mr. Agnelli Sr. was appreciative of Constantin's help with his indelicate situation and would certainly extend himself for Constantin's family. They could pull some strings and arrange an O visa."

Constantin didn't know what that was.

Dimitru explained it was a visa that applies to people with extraordinary abilities.

Always encouraging Dimitru to go into the family business, Mr. Agnelli Sr. tried to teach his son the ins and outs of getting things done internationally. It didn't hurt to be an intimate friend of the US ambassador and know the consul.

The young men opened up the computer and went to Google for the confirmation of their information."

It was there in black and white. The O Visa did apply to the skills that Mihaela had developed.

Dimitru was proud of the worldly knowledge that he had gained. Now he saw an application for what his father had shared with him. Constantin was delighted that one major problem could be solved. Mihaela needed to get her visa in

Bucharest, where it could be arranged. The Agnelli company didn't have the same level of influence in London.

Switching their conversation to the timetable Dimitru shared the progress that he had already made. He had rented a flat next to Mrs. French's house. As a cover story Mrs. French was told that Constantin's parents won a lottery and wanted to use their money to further educate their girls. That way she wouldn't be too curious. In addition, Mihaela was going to have a job in the Agnelli Oil Co. office as a translator, and she could stay in Bucharest at Dimitru's parents house. At home they had eight bedrooms and only three of them were being used."

Constantin finished the plan with the statement that he needed to accompany her from Bistriţa since his father would never let her travel alone

Constantin called his family that night and explained the new opportunity for Mihaela. After an hour of explanation, his mother still resisted his plan. Basically she was afraid, or didn't understand, how important this moment was. It was the beginning of the fulfillment of Matei's and Sophie's hopes, aspirations, and dreams of a far better life for their children. It was, however, very hard for them to trust and let go.

Finally, Matei said, OK she can fly alone. They arranged for Matei to take Mihaela to Cluj Napoca airport, so that she could fly to Bucharest. Now they needed Mihaela to agree.

She enthusiastically said, yes!

Matei demanded that Constantin promise to pick her up from the airport.

He reassured his parents that his plan would succeed and that he would be there for all of them, every step of the way.

Constantin called home with this offer after first making sure that his sister would be welcomed in Dimitru's house. Dimitru's father had also been totally cooperative with giving her a position in his company. The next morning, Mr. Agnelli Sr. called his friend at the US embassy and invited him to have lunch, which he accepted. Politically he was considered an important ally of United States' interests in Romania. During that lunch, Mr. Agnelli gave the the ambassador a rundown of the girl's linguistic ability, which really interested him. Timing is everything in life, and this was the right moment for a friendly Farsi speaker. He was aware that NATO was looking for someone with the ability to speak Farsi. The next step would be to supply the proper US department with her information. He then contacted the NATO representative, who needed someone with Farsi translation abilities. There was immediate interest in meeting this western friendly Farsi speaker to see if she could be useful in the delegation that they were currently organizing representing western interests.

Things started moving fast, and Constantin's adrenaline rush was evident. His senses heightened, and he had a sudden burst of energy. He breathed with intensity and felt stronger than ever. He was ready for his plan and formulating it as the events unfolded. The family though eager was fearful and unsure.

CHAPTER 26

GOOD-BYE, BISTRITA

Constantin was very protective of his precious sisters. Since Mihaela had never traveled alone or flown on a plane, he arrived early to the airport in Bucharest. The airport was quiet early on Saturday, when Constantin arrived at Bucharest Aurel Vlaicu airport.

With Mihaela leaving her father had decided to skip work. They had a lot of things to discuss. He had brought special foods and other treats from a market in Bistrita. To begin, they had an incredible breakfast. They had not eaten herring and feta cheese for such a long time. These were a delicacy to them. In addition Sophy had prepared a delicious *mameligue* (a corn-meal-based pasta-like meal), something all Romanians ate, mainly because it's inexpensive and delicious. He also brought the prized Kalamata olives and sour cream.

Loana said, "I can live happily forever with this type of meal."

They all laughed, and discussed Constantin's new, revised plan for Mihaela in Bucharest. He had arranged for her stay in Dimitru's home, and on Monday she was to meet one of the US embassy officers. Constantin had sent her some appropriate clothing to travel in. These included pants and a sweater-like shirt. This was quite a change since she had worn only long skirts or dresses. The other girls gave the family an update on their activities and preparations at the library. Daniela was picking at her hair and Sophy got angry at that and an argument ensued. Loana said that a new employee at the library returned from Australia and spoke to her in English. He wanted to take her to a dance, but her father wouldn't let her go. Constantin had reminded them to please hold off a little longer. He also said we can't take any chances on having a problem now. We are too close to the beginning of our new future."

Mother interjected. "So what happens to your father and me? Are you leaving us here alone? No plans for us? After all, we have done everything for all of you. Good-bye, and that's it?"

"Mother, please, how can you say that? As soon as we start with our first success, we will not leave you behind, we swear."

"Yes, that's all that young people do; they swear, to remember their parents but they make a new life and forget the loved ones of the past.

Feeling the heat of anger at their love being questioned, the question arose among the daughters, Well, Mother,

it's about time you told us about your family. No more secrets. And you too, Dad. This is our last get together here
in Romania. We will meet soon in another country with another life and no more poverty, so tell us about your past life.

CHAPTER 27

FLYING HIGH

Wow, there I was, on a Boeing 737—me, Mihaela. I couldn't believe it! It was so impressive, even though I know there are larger planes. It still amazes me that a huge piece of steel like that can lift off the ground. It was such a strange sensation as we lifted off. I have never felt anything like that before. The airport was breathtaking also. People rushing in all directions, and everyone seemed so comfortable with it. Where have I been? So this is life. The sight out the window was just amazing—I was flying through the clouds. How did they know where and how to land this giant plane? I can see that there are many wonderful things waiting for me in life now. It really is going to happen.

It was so special when Dimitru's driver came and picked us up at the airport. We drove to the Complex Mirano, a big mall where they had wonderful shops. We ran right through, and Constantin selected some wonderful clothing for me. We had a little bit of a hard time with the shoes. My taste was not as daring as Constantin's. At home as a child I wore shoes as infrequently as possible, and recently while going to the library each day, I only wore simple flats or pumps. It was a shopping spree. It was like a dream; if I saw it and liked it, we bought it. I knew from the magazines and the computer what women were wearing in the United Kingdom and the United States. We shopped for a few hours, and then we went to Dimitru's home. It was a gigantic, somewhat like I had seen in magazines at the library. So they do exist! Once there I met his mother and father. They seemed to like me right away. I felt they were very nice, and after all this kindness, how could I feel anything but warmth towards them? They must be wonderful people to do all of this for our family. We were all hungry, and we sat down to dinner. It was like being in the hotel restaurant. Everything was beautiful, and the food was delicious. Some of the dishes I asked about, and some of them they explained, seeing that I did not recognize them. There were so many forks and spoons and knives, I just followed what they did. Dimitru's mother said to me during the meal that we should go upstairs later and get better acquainted. I never realized that she was going to share her makeup and cosmetics with me. She even showed me how to apply them and use them for the greatest impact. When I came downstairs, all the men were taken with my new appearance.

All of our interaction was in English from the minute we entered the house, and I did fine. I'm sure they were helping me to get ready for my interview at the US embassy. Later they reviewed what I should ask, as well as how I should answer the questions that would be put to me. They were clear: "Do not ask to visit the United States unless it is suggested by the embassy officer." I was to keep my Romanian ID and passport with me, and I would see what came of the interview. My life was happening fast and furious. Mr. Agnelli, Dimitru's dad, did explain that I was the sister of Dimitru's best friend. With all this going on, I surprisingly felt calm. Mrs. Agnelli took me upstairs again after dessert, and we tore into the new clothes to find the right outfit for the interview. Dimitru commented to his father that he had not seen his mother so excited and cooperative with anyone before. Mr. Agnelli said, "It seems this is the daughter she never had."

CHAPTER 28

SHE IS A FIND

onstantin drove Mihaela to the embassy after repeating instructions on how she should respond, in addition to whatever else came to his mind that he thought would be helpful. Mihaela was surprisingly quite relaxed. The night before was filled with dreams, thoughts, fear, and most of all excitement. She could not wait for morning to come and life to begin. It was like being born!

She was so beautiful, she was sure to impress, especially if the interviewer was a man. At exactly nine o'clock, she walked through the heavily guarded security at the embassy and was met by a female security agent. She was led to a hall with office doors one after the other. They walked quickly, passing door after door, until she arrived at the door marked Lieutenant Mike Fellows. He greeted her warmly, and he started speaking Farsi, which she didn't expect. However, she was able to answer with ease in the basic language. The night before she had memorized a friendly poem in Farsi that she thought was appropriate, and he was impressed. Seamlessly, he then spoke to her in Arabic, and she also responded to his statement appropriately. He then went back to English, and the interview began. It was clear that her facility with language matched her beauty, and he thought to himself, "She is a grand slam home run!"

Lieutenant Mike Fellows was thoroughly impressed with this very young Romanian woman that he had been asked to interview by the ambassador himself. It was suggested that she might fit into the multilingual program. It began as a directive from upstairs, yet it turned into a very interesting morning. She was beautiful, which began the exchange on a very positive note. She seemed very cooperative and open in the interview. He had a feeling of her naivety and her awe with the surroundings. The offices were impressive, and the uniform did the trick as well. She did not present credentials of advanced schooling, but she was able to keep up with English and three other languages that were tested. She answered the initial questions with such clarity and understanding of the subjects that he was literarily speechless. For a linguist that is saying something.

When he asked her what her objective was in coming to the embassy, she said, "Since I am able to speak several languages, I may be able to help the United States or other NATO embassies, and they might give me employment." She was very articulate in everything she said, and honest. He knew that since he had to do a background check as part of the routine for admittance into his department. Nothing was negative except the fact that she was a good student from a small city with a rural education system in Romania and had never had a job. She presented her Romanian ID and a birth certificate and had only two references, the ambassador himself and Mr. Agnelli, who was someone very friendly to US interests.

At first, he didn't know what type of entry job to offer this seemingly accomplished young woman. Then he remembered he had seen a memorandum from Washington. They desperately needed translators, especially in Farsi and Arabic. The memo stated "Urgent Need" in red letters. This girl was so beautiful, he didn't feel like sending her to Washington to be trained there. He felt like keeping her here in this small embassy. That was selfish; she could be of use in several government entities in Washington. However, he decided that a video interview was in order. It was sent out to several departments and to the ambassador as well. There was no doubt that they would grab her immediately.

CHAPTER 29

THE PIECES FIT TOGETHER

As life happens, there was an incident with Iran and the United States that turned into a hot issue. There would be a showdown on oil interests and the use of the money that the oil raises. Iran was secretly pursuing nuclear capability. The world was very concerned about these developments. Meanwhile back in Bucharest Lieutenant Fellows received several responses to his video interview from different agencies. To make things more tense, an Iranian ship off the coast of Turkey in the Black Sea confronted an American ship. Suddenly, both Farsi and other linguistics were needed by the US government. Coming from a neutral country like Romania was a benefit as a cover. Knowing how to navigate the red tape, Lieutenant Fellows contacted the US counsel general directly. He wanted to inquire as to the type of visa available for Mihaela to become part of an agency. He was told that the EB1 visa was the one that applied to exceptional talent. Lieutenant Fellows confirmed all of her information, and with mixed feelings of sadness, shared this young treasure with another agency.

He called Mihaela's cell phone and gave her an immediate appointment for the next day. He followed that with a memo to the ambassador. In the chain of events Mr. Agnelli was called by his friend the Ambassador who told him the interview had gone well, and that she would be offered an EB1 Visa leading to a permanent visa to the United States and a good job with the government, after a six month trial in the field. This good news was shared with Dumitru and he informed Constantin of the outcome. Things were going so well, they needed to get together and see what to do next for Mihaela.

Constantin reminded himself that the objective of all this must not be forgotten or delayed. She was going to the US to meet a billionaire and become wealthy in whatever manner. He secretly thought; *will this job she has been offered in any way impede or delay our overall objective? When she arrives in the US, we need to be in constant contact. How will we achieve this? I hope she is not sent to another country. How do we avoid her falling in love with someone at work? Oh, we have so many obstacles that could derail our ultimate goals. How should I proceed? This is something that I cannot share with Dimitru. He has never been crushingly poor, and this is one thing that he could never understand.*

CHAPTER 30

THE RAPID PACE OF CHANGE

Mihaela's appointment at the embassy was very early in the morning. She put on the most appropriate outfit that was bought in the shopping spree. Having read so many magazines it was easy to make a reasonable judgement of what to wear. Prior to going she reviewed all the details with both Constantin and Dimitru. Her expectation was to meet with the same lieutenant, but she was shown into the office of the counsel general, Mr. Best, for her second screening interview. He had explained that what was needed was her Romanian passport and passport photos. In addition there were several forms to fill out requiring a lot of information about herself, her parents, and siblings. Her job would involve high-security issues, and therefore there would be Homeland Security forms as well. They would need information about her maternal and paternal families.

Hearing these informational requirements concerned her greatly. These were aspects of her history that she knew nothing about. Being bright, she decided to listen and not comment on all the requirements being presented.

Mr. Best told her that instructions were received to speed up her application. A person with her linguistic talent was needed immediately. He continued to take a complete set of fingerprints. Next, he had her sign a consent form and acknowledgment of understanding the instructions. She was given a telephone number to call as soon as she had everything ready. When the meeting was over, Lieutenant Fellows appeared and invited her for coffee. He introduced her to other embassy officials. She was apparently something special to them, a very young Romanian with special talents and abilities. Her broad range of linguistics was rare, and they all wanted to meet her. One of them made the observation that they had never seen such a combination of intelligence and beauty. After small talk and evident flirtation by some of the male officers, she left with a promise to return soon. Mihaela was nervous and in emotional distress.

Is this the end of my journey? How am I going to get credible information on my relatives, and what will they find if they delve into my extended family history? I'm sure that there are dark secrets or I would have more information about my relatives. Everything is happening so quickly.

CHAPTER 31

A LIGHT SHINES ON THE DARKNESS

Constantin said, "I knew things were going too smoothly. Now what do we do next? First things first."

He called Loana and told her to go to their father's shop with Daniela and give the cell phone to her father. Constantin spoke very deliberately. "I need to speak to him urgently."

She said, "We can't leave the library alone because Dad would not permit it." Every day he would pick them up at six o'clock.

Constantin then said, "I need you to do this now, no questions, please. Take the bus and go now!"

The sisters felt the gravity of his voice and took off immediately. When they arrived at the shop, their father was shocked. "What happened?"

They immediately called Constantin, and he explained

everything to them. At this point their father had no choice; he told them everything he knew about Sophie's family. He shared the names of all the brothers and their cousins they had never met. Matei felt they were thieves and most likely on police lists as known Communist sympathizers. He also explained that he believed that probably many of the relatives had jail records in Hungary. Constantin then asked his dad for the same kind of information about his family in Constanta. Searching his memory and trying to be as honest as he could, he went into as much detail as he knew. Everything he shared was written down on the immigration forms as honestly as they could. They knew that omissions could not be made. As bad as the information was, any lie would be detrimental to Mihaela.

As Mihaela, and Constantin began filling out the necessary forms Dimitru insisted on getting Mr. Agnelli's advice. They were reluctant to involve him even more, but he was more than willing. Mr. Agnelli was quite interested in all that Dimitru had planned, maybe too interested. Constantin wondered why a man of such wealth and influence was helping his son's friend in such a gamble. Constantin did not realize that Mr. Agnelli admired him and his brash and aggressive style. It reminded him of himself all those years ago. He was happy to see Dimitru involved with creative thought, and life accomplishment. This was the spark his son had needed. Mr. Agnelli also was feeling invigorated by the mystery and intrigue.

After a brief discussion, they all agreed that the

information required should be as exact as possible. It needed to be completed as soon as possible. In less than ten days, Dimitru was to fly to London with his sisters to set things in motion with Mrs. French. That meant that the Brazilian passport they had bought should be discarded. It needed to disappear and not complicate matters. That afternoon, Mihaela was to go to the Romanian passport office. She brought a letter of recommendation on Mr. Agnelli's company stationary. It stated that a passport was required immediately for an employee of the company. It was the only way of getting things done fast. At the same time, Dimitru called Daniella and had her go to the local passport office with Loana. They went with passport pictures to get passports as soon as possible. If necessary, he would send his father's company letter. Things started moving very quickly.

With a feeling of excitement in the house, Dimitru's mother got involved. She took Mihaela shopping for some additional clothing. Mihaela had little or no experience with the art of flirting, which was happening now that she was out of her sheltered life. Mrs. Agnelli saw it everywhere they went, and Mihaela had no idea of what a stir she caused when she walked in. She had read novels and remembered descriptions of these situations, and she had many discussions with her sisters about sexuality and its consequences. However, she never personalized the information. Dimitru's mother, observing her innocence, gave her a talk on how to fend off unwanted approaches. She needed to know how to deal with approaches that were acceptable. This was like having a daughter for the first time. That afternoon Mihaela called the US counsel to tell him she had everything he had asked for. This affirmed to the counsel how efficient and thorough she was and that his judgement about her was correct. He gave her an appointment for nine o'clock the next morning.

9 AM came very quickly. Mihaela was overwhelmed with the speed of events but had the presence of mind to say to the ambassador, "Could I make a written statement accompanying my Homeland Security questionnaire?"

He said, "Of course, it's your right."

The application went in with a handwritten letter. Looking at the letter after she left, the ambassador saw that her mother's family were estranged from the moment that her parents had first met. That neither she nor her siblings had any idea of their whereabouts and had never met them or ever communicated with them. This was a new wrinkle in the plan in order to protect her against any investigative procedure. Her father's family were much safer because, although she had never met them, they communicated sometimes with her father. They were good, normal people, according to him. Mihaela didn't want anything to block her part of the plan. Life was just beginning for her; all that came before was leading up to these developments. The consul sent her Romanian passport for processing and said that a provisional visa would be given. It would be ratified after Homeland Security authorized her application.

Mihaela's only comment was, "Why are they in such a rush?" She knew why she was in a hurry, but didn't get their urgency.

The consul said, "I follow orders and I don't know the motive."

She waited in a room alone at first and was then approached by the lieutenant. He said, "Would you be ready to travel to Washington in two days? A training course is to begin this weekend, and it is part of your future job requirement."

Overwhelmed with this information, she was honest with him and shared that she had never traveled out of Romania before. Lieutenant Fellows thought about how young, inexperienced, and beautiful she was. He tried to reassure her and told her not to worry, that he was assigned to travel with her and would introduce her to America. In two days she would be on a plane for the other side of the world. She would be with a man that she did not know, working for a country that she had only heard about. She would be staying in a hotel room all by herself, trying to function in a foreign language while translating several other foreign languages. Life was amazing. Since Constantin came home with Dimitru, everything had changed! That also meant that she would not see her sisters or parents or brother until a future date. What a mix of emotions!

CHAPTER 32

MOVING ON

Constantin confirmed that Mihaela was to leave for the United States. His plan was beginning with a few changes already. The next part involved Daniela and Loana. He gave them all the pertinent information about their trip to Bucharest then London. For the plan to be effective, they had to look the part.

Constantin said, "Buy some new clothes like the ones that you have seen worn in the magazines or on the Internet, to travel with." He suggested they go with their mom and dad to the Comalin store in Pta Centrale. It was a relatively new store with modern Western clothing. "Buy shoes and the entire outfit. You need to buy everything from underwear to jackets, and while you are at it, get rid of your sandals. I know that neither of you have ever worn high heels, so buy two pairs of low heels each. Buy them and try them around the house so you can learn to balance. You will need pocketbooks and wallets. Go to the makeup department and have them teach you how to apply the cosmetics, then buy the products. Pay attention when they are teaching you. When you are at the store, see how the other woman wear their hair. I have a beauty salon that I want you both to go to. I left you each a credit card with your name on it. You can spend whatever you need to accomplish this learning experience. Go early in the day, and take your time to absorb the details. Your futures may depend on it. This is your first step, even before your training starts."

They were to continue reading all they could find about London and the customs of the English. Dimitru had rented a small, furnished apartment close to Notting Hill. It was a two-bedroom, and they had it for three months. They would receive airline tickets to meet in Bucharest and from there continue to London together with Constantin and Dimitru.

The parents were very nervous about the possibility of something going wrong. They knew that their daughters were naive and they were concerned since several important experiences were about to happen. Though they did not physically appear to be of Gypsy origin their people had been stereotyped and discriminated against for many years. It was for this reason that Matei had separated his children from their neighbors and classmates. His family were unlike most Gypsies. He didn't allow his children to use profanity or derogatory language. They also didn't harass others. Not all their neighbors were the same. There are over 11 million people called Romani (Gypsy), yet his family was special. He was proud of his heritage but knew that it was a challenge in the outside world. It was originally thought that his people came from Egypt. From the reading that he had done, he found that his forefathers had a Y chromosome and mitochondrial DNA that are found only in Southeast Asia. They migrated from India to Europe. Unlike most Gypsies that are dark skinned, the Woods were clear skinned and had mestizo characteristics. Maybe that's why all the family were very good looking and different from the traditional appearance.

Matei and Sophy Woods needed to prepare for the absence of their children. They all would be gone at once. They had a share of the plan too, and theirs began right away as well. It was their job to start telling whoever they talked to that they were going to move to Constanta, to Matei's family. They felt that would be a reasonable cover story. The parents also believed they would move after the success of Constantin's plan.

CHAPTER 33

IS THIS FOR REAL?

Mihaela pondered; *Constantin, Mom, and particularly Dad want this great life for us, so I guess I do too. OK, I'll start this adventure, and here we go. The lieutenant and I arrived in Vienna. During the flight out of Bucharest, he started to explain to me about life in the United States. He discussed what was probably going to be my job. In doing so, he said the first two weeks I would be attending a policy seminar. And although my English was not fluent yet that I should stick to it and I would soon understand everything. It was hard for me to follow his words, but I was trying. He used phrases that I had never heard before and that did not follow word-by-word meanings. "Stick to it" I assumed meant keep trying, and that is what I intended on doing. Even though this was more challenging than anything I had tried before, if this is what my family wanted for me, I'd do it! However, here I was, on the plane, and I wanted to share it with my sisters as we had always done in the past. My sisters and brother were my best friends. They*

were my only real friends, and now I was alone. The lieutenant was not at liberty to give more information until I was totally cleared by Homeland Security.

The flight was impressive, amazing, and scary at the same time. This was my first time on a large transatlantic airplane, but little did I know that this would become as usual for me as brushing my teeth in the morning. In the airport in Vienna, we had time to eat lunch, and that also was a first for me. I had been to a restaurant in a hotel in Bistriţa with Constantin and Dimitru, but this was something special. I had no idea what to order, and the lieutenant suggested that I try something that he liked very much. I had a Japanese dish called sushi, and it was totally different from the food that I had eaten in Romania. I could imagine that I would find many surprises in the near future. Dimitru told me not to show surprise at anything. He told me to avoid showing my ignorance of the modern world. I decided to do that. I needed to look around and watch the other people and the lieutenant and see what they did. I saw that they used both the fork and knife to push the food on the plate. They dabbed their mouths repeatedly with the napkin. I also noticed that they looked at one another while eating and stopped and talked in between. This was going to be quite a challenge. My new shoes were tight on the toes, and my new clothes showed my figure but hugged me constantly. These were all new feelings, but strange, not painful.

After eating, we boarded our flight to Washington, DC. This was my third time at flying, but it still felt weird to be lifted up from under my seat and see the land grow distant under me *through the window. The lieutenant suggested it would be ideal to sleep because of the six-hour time difference when we arrived in Washington. How could I sleep? I was so excited, and there were so many new experiences. I even ate a meal on the plane. The airline people who took care of us on the trip were so nice. I still could not understand why the time would be different when we landed. The time had passed while we were in the plane; hadn't the time passed on land as well? New ideas, new experiences, what next? So I had to rest as much as possible, but that was going to be difficult. I had too many things on my mind.*

One of them was my worry over my parents staying alone for the first time in Bistriţa. I was also worried about something that was a secret from my parents. Loana had been having an issue with Joko. He was a young man who was in love with her, even though they had only spoken once. He seemed to follow her everywhere. When we were in the library, he was always near the library. He was tall and strong looking, but we knew very little about him. He was not a Gypsy. He was half French and half Romanian. Joko was studying auto mechanics at a local garage. His family was not poor, but that's all we knew. I knew that Loana was interested and flattered. He wrote love notes to her and left them where we could find them. He was relentless in his quest for her to give him a hint of interest. I think she started to wear down and was starting to smile when she saw him. Things were changing just in time, as she would be leaving town and disappearing from the life she would have had with him. She was moving into a new, exciting, powerful life far away. Just in time!

Ten hours later we were in Washington. I was driven to the hotel in a huge, beautiful car with a driver. Passing through the city was amazing. I had never seen so many cars in one place. The roads were full. We passed huge buildings and so many people. Everyone was dressed so differently from what I was used to. The highways and roads were so smooth. The driver opened the car door when we arrived at the hotel. I thought it was a palace. The gold and stone front shone in the daylight. The lieutenant carried my bag in, and I walked into a huge beautiful room that was the lobby. It was decorated like a dream room. Marble and polished wood were everywhere. I needed to show this to my sisters and parents. They wouldn't believe where I was now! I had stepped into a fantasy. The lieutenant helped me check in, and then we took a beautiful glass elevator to the floor upstairs. My room was larger than my house at home. This was just for me? We all lived together at home. The person who brought up my suitcase showed me the room. I had to stop and try to take it all in. He spoke of the air conditioning thermostat and showed me where it was. Then he gave me the TV remote and next showed me the view of the park outside the windows. We were on the twentieth floor. I felt like I was back on the airplane. Last of all he told me that the phone on the bed stand could be used to call for room service twenty-four hours a day, and they would bring me whatever I needed. This was too much! Could this be true? I needed to play with these new items, but there was only a short night, and I needed to be ready at seven thirty in the morning to be taken to the seminar. I had arrived in America! This was the beginning of my new amazing life!

CHAPTER 34

THE FIRST MAJOR TEST

We had a rushed meal at the hotel—I was not used to these meals. They served bagels and coffee and many things I had not seen before. In Bistriţa we had bread and sometimes milk when it was available. A milkman used to come by with a cow, and my mother would run down the hill with a bucket and milk the cow. That's how we sometimes had milk. Since our house didn't have electricity, we didn't have anything that needed to be kept cool in the summer. In the winter we didn't need a refrigerator. I had such an urge to call my sisters and see how they were doing. I also wanted to tell them about my adventures and the discoveries I had made. I couldn't! Constantin told me not to call unless there was an emergency. But I spoke to all of them all day every day in the past. This was going to be lonely. I had to do this all by myself. I couldn't even ask Constantin a question if I needed to. I was very clearly instructed not to trust anyone. Here I was, all alone. I ate the food and started the day.

A car came to pick me up. My brother had bought me a watch in Bucharest, so I had no problem being on time. The hotel room also had a small box displaying the hour. The room had a big TV, just like in Dimitru's house. I needed to learn how to use a very complicated TV control.

I was signed in and given an electronic badge at this gigantic building on Pennsylvania Avenue. The president's White House was also on this street. I had been reading everything Dimitru's mother had given me about the city of Washington. These were important meetings, and it was like being back in school. I listened to several speakers on the art of translation and interpretation in Farsi, Arabic, and other languages. There were over two hundred people like me. I spoke to some of them during the coffee break. What a surprise! My parents would be shocked; I now liked coffee. While sipping another cup of coffee, I was approached by one of the other girls. She was Italian but spoke Farsi because her father was born in Iran. Her father had passed away a long time ago, yet she had learned Farsi as a child. I remembered Constantin's words to "trust no one," yet three young men attempted to invite me to lunch. Everyone was new and I guess as afraid as I was. I decided to stay with the Italian girl.

We were then fingerprinted again and photographed at different angles. One of the attendees asked what company or government entity we were in. He was told that each one eventually would be assigned to one of the many high-security agencies of US government. I felt part of the group, and my English was as good or better than most. I knew that

this was step one in the plan for the life that was being im-
plemented for me. I was happy with my first day. I made it
through, but how sweet it would have been to tell the family
about my first day. That was never to be again, not in the way
it was. Life had already changed forever. That night I was
so emotionally exhausted and physically tired I fell right to
sleep. Maybe it was what they all had been talking about over
coffee—jet lag, a new phrase for me to remember.

On the third day of the seminar, I was interviewed by one
of the security officers. He apparently had all my information, and after seeing me said, "I'll interview her!" Following
a conversation in English, he gave me a tape of two males having a conversation. They spoke in Farsi, concerning money
to be transferred to a numbered account in Luxembourg. I
was given fifteen minutes to listen to the tape and give him
a synopsis of the content. I knew that this would be a very
important test. Listening intently to the tape, the males spoke
at a rapid pace, as native speakers do. They had an inflection
that usually indicates the northern part of Iran. There were
shortened sentences and clipped words. I knew most of it and
guessed the rest. What made it even more difficult was the
fact that they did not give paper to write anything down. I
have an excellent memory. That was my gift therefore I was
able to master several languages.

The interviewer watched me intently as I worked, he was
thinking; s*he is beautiful and smart. What a combination!*

Then onto the next step, which was to write a letter in
Farsi on a computer. Here I had no experience and had never

written on a computer in Farsi before. Hesitating I remembered Constantin's order to "never let anyone know that you don't know." I was given thirty minutes to write a letter to a museum in Teheran. In order to collect my thoughts, I requested a bathroom break, which I was given. In the ladies' room I thought long and hard and realized, what was the worst that could happen? Returning refreshed, it still wasn't easy for me. Luck was on my side, and the tester liked the outcome. I also noticed that the tester liked me. For the first time, I truly felt the power of my femininity.

I suspect he did not speak or write Farsi, but I gave him the impression that I was an expert. He asked me if I was ready to accept a job in the agency. I answered, "That was why I came to Washington."

He gave me an appointment for the next morning with a Mr. Clancy. He said, "Now that the interview is over, may I have your cell phone number so that I can show you our wonderful city?"

I smiled, and then I mentioned that I had just arrived in the United States. I had no local information, address, or bank accounts, and therefore I had no cell phone number to share. I knew that I had to be very careful and not insult or reject him in any way. He was the key to my future. He saw my pertinent information on the computer and told me that I would be issued a government ID. In addition I would receive a cell phone with international capabilities. He included the sly comment that he would look forward to hearing from me as he handed me his card. I smiled again.

Then he continued by saying, "You will have an account opened in a Washington bank, and an immediate salary deposit will be made, so you can use that for expenses. Finally, you will be given a debit card and credit card."

I was not to comment to anyone, including my seminar friends, about this, and I was free to go. Since I could not hold back, I asked if Homeland Security had approved my application. He said he did not know, but he was sure I wouldn't be offered a job if I hadn't been checked and approved. I also asked about my visa status. Again he sounded very official, and he said that he didn't know but that he would ask. He left me with the words, "Call me in the office here tomorrow, and I'll try to find out for you."

She would be informed ASAP since she might have to travel overseas. When she left she was exhausted. All of her intellectual, social, and feminine skills had been tested. She passed, but it took a lot. She was not happy that she might have to leave this wonderful, beautiful, exciting city for "overseas." More changes that she was not ready for. Wasn't this enough?

CHAPTER 35

SO CLOSE YET SO FAR

Back in Bistrita an absence is felt. A young man named Joko knew that something was wrong. He recalled in his mind; *I first met the three girls when Constantin went to a soccer game in the upper-grade-school stadium. We knew one another casually, and he would say, "Hi, Joko, how are you doing?" I didn't think much about him until I saw his beautiful sisters, particularly Loana. She was fifteen then, and Loana was so beautiful, I couldn't take my eyes off her. After finding out that her father made her totally inaccessible to anyone, I attempted to befriend her brother. Suddenly, I would engage him about sports and school. It was a little awkward because the year above didn't usually befriend the year below; however, it worked because he was athletic like me. I didn't give him enough credit. He picked up on my interest in Loana. I thought I was subtle, but he was clever.*

From then on he remained polite, but I never again could get near him. Lately, things had become really strange. Suddenly they seemed to have a lot of money. They went to a store and brought new clothes. I saw them downtown near the garage where I am learning my trade. Another day, I saw that they went to a hotel in a fancy car with their parents. These are people who had no money. Maybe they are setting up to marry off one of the beautiful girls to a rich man. What made it even stranger was that Constantin, their brother, was the driver. Maybe he connected with some kind of a big job, or maybe he had some underworld connections. You don't just show up with a car and money for clothes out of nowhere. This represented a lot of money. It was a Lexus. I am familiar with the brand, and it costs a fortune. We don't have many of those in our city. It definitely wasn't his.

Lately, I have seen that they now travel by bus without their father. That is strange, but they are all together, and I cannot approach Loana, even though I want to. Another strange thing is going on. Loana has been talking to an Asian woman. I don't know if she is Chinese or Korean. We don't have many people like that in town. What does she want with her or from her? A lot of strange things are happening, but I still would love to get close to my Loana. I speak a little English since I need to study car manuals and most are in English. I have seen and heard Loana and her sisters study English at the library. What do they need that for? They need a husband from a good family, who has a good job. I am that guy. I intend to approach her the next time I see her. I want to ask if my father can contact her father to arrange a get-together. She is a Gypsy; they should jump at the chance to have a good family like mine. Since

Constantin has not been around, I can't even use him to try to connect with her. School has ended, and I'm at the garage all day. It's near the library, but I can't just storm in there and talk to her. The only way is through our fathers. I'm counting on my dad to make the case for me. He says I should pick a girl with money, but I only want Loana. I need to convince him to make the call. He is stalling, hoping I'll meet someone else. I don't want to miss her.

CHAPTER 36

OBSESSION

We have only one son, and to both of us, Dimitru is our life! We were so lucky to have been able to have him. We thanked God, and his birth gave us faith. He turned into a very popular and outgoing student. Though we are his parents, the evaluation of his teachers and others indicate that he is a genius in mathematics. That is just like my husband, who is also gifted in math. That's why our family has been so successful in businesses, which we have spread to many countries. We didn't want our son to go to MIT, which is half the world away. It's nice to have him in our home as long as possible. His brilliance in mathematics goes beyond that; he sees possibilities and potential in life. He will be the catalyst for the whole family's further success. He has many acquaintances, and girls go crazy over him. It's not only because of our wealth, even though we are wealthy, it's his good looks and pleasant personality. I learned from my parents the importance of choosing the right person to marry. My husband chose me as his wife and made *my life. Therefore, we are preoccupied with who will share his future and who he will choose. Dimitru has a clear idea of what he wants in his life.*

Almost two years now, he met a young man at his Institute who he immediately liked and trusted. Reflecting his kindness he offered to help him and to have him stay here with the family. At first I was concerned, and I consulted with my husband. We thought that it might be a good idea because Dimitru didn't have siblings. Dimitru gravitated to this young man Constantin and it was going to be temporary. We agreed to his request because his brilliance does extend to life and people. We met Constantin, and we thought he was really special, similar to Dimitru. We saw in him the same light as our son; he was too good to be true. Constantin needed polishing of his skills for society, and Dimitru had those skills.

Constantin also needed to understand money and what it can buy as well as how to use it effectively. Dimitru needed a true friend on his level, and the boys were kindred spirits. In no time Constantin was one of the household. Dimitru was so happy to have him, and they became shadows of each other. They were both excellent students, and now our son had a substitute brother.

Dimitru got very involved in Constantin's plan to get his family out of extreme poverty. He participated in formulating all kinds of plans on how to proceed. Then they planned a car trip to visit Constantin's family. When they returned his father and I noticed an extreme change in our son. He was uneasy; we know that he didn't sleep much and became involved even more

114

with Constantin's plan. One morning I got up very early. As a mother you feel these things in your bones, and I noticed my son sitting alone in the den in the dark. I asked him, "What is happening to you? Since you returned from Bistriţa, you have changed. You have never been like this. Son, we don't have secrets; please tell me. We are worried."

"OK, Mother, I will tell you. But swear to me that Constantin won't hear anything about this. It is very important to me."

She agreed since her curiosity was way beyond normal. What she didn't know was that her husband had followed her to see what was happening at four o'clock in the morning.

Dimitru said, "When I met Constantin's family, I fell totally in love with his sister, Daniela. I am obsessed with thoughts of her. I have never met someone like her, and I can't stop thinking about Daniela. I have taken a picture of the sisters with my phone and blew the image up so you could see her beauty."

Now his father joined the conversation, and his parents looked at his eyes and saw his passion for her.

"It is very important Constantin doesn't find out until the right time."

Mrs. Agnelli asked, "Does she know?"

"I don't think so. I've never spoken to her alone. I don't think she noticed my stare and my nervousness when I looked at her."

Continuing, mother said, "Are you sure it's not a simple infatuation?"

"Yes, I'm sure. She is the most incredible person I have ever met."

Dimitru's parents were not convinced it was love, but they understood that their son had entered a new phase of life. They also knew that his intelligence was beyond book smarts. However, in the arena of love, he was a novice. This young woman was strikingly beautiful, but they wanted to get to know her before they supported his "love" for her.

CHAPTER 37

THE SPY WHO DID NOT HAVE TO SPY

Mihaela knew that today would be fundamental to her future in the United States. She got up very early and went to have her breakfast. This hotel had a buffet breakfast. It was more food than she had ever seen in one place at one time. It looked to her like the market from home. You could take whatever you wanted and as much as you wished. This was a dream come true. She controlled her response and acted like everyone else. All the products were labeled, but many items she did not recognize. She managed and ate like a queen. After all, this was her second day.

Then she went to the front desk after she was informed that an envelope had been left for her. She went back to her room, and to her surprise she found exactly what she was told the day before. An activated iPhone was there, containing a list of instructions. Preinstalled important numbers to call and a password were included, but it advised that she activate the fingerprint ID app. Constantin had shown her some of these things quickly. Still she would have to ask some questions or push some buttons and try. She also found a debit card, credit card, and a small five-check folder, all in her name. In a separate envelope, she found a US government ID, valid for ten years. She was to appear at her appointment at ten o'clock that morning.

She asked herself, "What happened? Why after two days in the seminar was I taken out and hired, when I had no real professional training in translations of any type?" She assumed that there was more than just translating. This made her nervous, and she had a strong urge to use her new phone to call Constantin. She had his phone number in Romania. In two days he was supposed to leave for London, then his telephone number would change, causing her to lose contact. Everything was happening at lightning speed.

Feeling lost, she went to the lobby and spoke to one of the valets. He had a Romanian name, Radu. Mihaela asked him if he knew how to operate an Apple phone. He took out his iPhone 7 and offered to help with hers. Taking a chance, and wanting the feeling of home, she started speaking Romanian to him. He smiled and was very impressed that he encountered such a beautiful woman and that she was Romanian. He told her that in five minutes he had a fifteen minute break. Then, he could teach her everything about the phone. He loved that phone, and his grandson had taught him everything. She agreed to meet him at a coffee shop in front of the hotel. By now it was eight o'clock, and she had time until her appointment.

She met Radu, and he bought two coffees and helped her apply the touch password. Then he showed her how to use the apps, and he activated "WhatsApp." He explained how to call Romania for free from anywhere in the world using the application. The intensive lesson went on as he taught her how to put contacts in and establish an e-mail address. She had to have one in order to have an Apple ID because that's how Apple works. Quickly, they established the easiest method would be to use her name and a number in a Gmail account. He proceeded to show her how to call her brother and placed his own information in contacts under the *R's* for Radu. Next he jotted down her information, and he had to return to work. She thanked him and then returned to her room.

She was armed with newfound knowledge about the phone. Understanding that the Wi-Fi in the hotel was fabulous and free, she was going to take advantage of that. So she pushed the phone icon in WhatsApp, and magic occurred. Constantin answered! She told him everything that had occurred, and she couldn't believe how easily she could reach him and that this was free.

He told her to be careful and that she had to find out her immigration status. He also cautioned her that if the job description was dangerous, she could refuse. She shouldn't go to a dangerous country. "If possible, stay in the US," he said, but now they both knew they could communicate whenever they wished to. Constantin warned, "I don't want you to have problems since you might work for a security agency. They are probably very suspicious of new employees."

She sent him Radu's telephone number and explained who he was. Radu had downloaded several important apps like the taxi service Ubcr and had placed her credit-card information on the app. She decided to take an Uber to the building where her ten o'clock appointment would be. In the envelope she received, she was told that the previous car service from the day before was not going to continue. She arrived on time at the address she gave to the driver. It was a large office building that did not look governmental. Once there, she walked into the office on the twenty-first floor and then was shown into a very modern room looking toward a large park. She still didn't know what agency wanted to interview her. There were no signs on the office door. The receptionist was an older woman with a distinct grin and Asian features. Mihaela waited and after fifteen minutes was advised that the interviewer was delayed in a meeting. She was offered coffee. It seemed that everyone drank coffee in Washington. At home, I always chose warm cow milk since we never drank coffee. I had read that coffee was also popular in the more educated middle-class homes in Romania.

The officer came in and excused himself, and then to my surprise, spoke to me in Romanian. He told me he would be my direct boss and case officer. Since I was not a US citizen, I couldn't officially work in that governmental agency. Yet he continued to say that he was authorized to have me work as a contractor for the agency. He asked me if I had received everything he sent to the hotel. I nodded. He told me about my immigration status. I was given an immediate O visa for my outstanding abilities with languages. In five years I could naturalize and become a United States citizen.

He explained the reason why everything had been done in such a rush. A Romanian delegation was going to visit Iran in three days. I was to accompany the delegation and keep an open eye, informing him every day of any suspicious activity. No one was to know of this agency contract. I would be sent as part of the Romanian government group. My case manager continued to say that I would be the only one that understood Farsi, and my mission would be to listen in on the Iranian plans without them knowing. They were all experts from the Romanian petroleum industry. The delegation was invited to visit the Iranian energy installations.

Mihaela was going to act as a new reporter for the *Romanian Petroleum Monthly Digest*. This was a brand-new company set up by the agency there in Washington. It was a safe cover for her to be brought along. She was given a folder with a small computer and made-up information to support the cover identity. The case manager added that the O visa was not placed on her Romanian passport.

"We managed to avoid the immigration-officer stamp, upon your entrance to the US. The Iranians won't see a United States immigration stamp on your passport. Your contract says you will be paid two hundred thousand dollars a year, minus income taxes. All expenses can be placed on your credit or debit card. We will pay everything. Your bank account is from an international bank in Romania, so it is no problem. We voided your payment to Uber this morning. There is no evidence of its use in the United States. Your new ID will have to be left in a safety deposit box, which we opened in a bank in Bucharest. It is in your name also, and this is the password that you need to add. The ID tag that you will leave in safekeeping is your proof and guarantee that we have given you the O visa. When you return to the US after this assignment, you will need to retrieve the ID to legally enter as an O-visa holder. Therefore, you will fly back through Bucharest. The immigration officer will scan your ID and will know you are a government-contracted agent. I know that this is a lot on short notice, but do you understand?"

"Yes."

"Your flight to Vienna leaves at two thirty, and then to Bucharest. Our people will meet you in Bucharest and set up your Romanian delegation first pre-trip meeting. Please buy clothes in Bucharest. In Iran women dress differently, as you probably know. Our people will help you and give you reporter credentials. So, have you decided?"

"Do I have a choice?"

"Yes, but I want you to know this is not dangerous. Our agent at the embassy will give you all the information. Call Radu."

What a shock that was, Radu. What a stroke of luck to have chosen him to befriend. Now I know that you never know who anyone really is working for!

CHAPTER 38

ENDINGS/BEGINNINGS: LOANA

Dear Diary,

So many new things are happening to all of us. I don't know how my brother's plans are going to work. He is relying totally on his friend's promise to finance his plan. I have followed his instructions to the letter. My English has really improved; I practice every day with the internet courses at the library. Lately I watch at least one movie in English without reading the Romanian subtitles. I have no problem at all understanding, nor does my sister Daniela.

Now that Mihaela is in the United States, only Daniela is at the library with me. Due to so many last-minute arrangements, my father doesn't mind when we travel alone on the bus. We aren't really alone; Joko follows us almost every day. I know he is very interested in me. I have grown accustomed to him always being around and sometimes I worry when I don't see him. He works and must study. Sometimes I feel I want to be with him.

It might interfere with my brother's plan, and I don't want to ruin his dream for us. We must all cooperate to save us from our sad life.

In a few days, we will be leaving for England, and I just finished talking to my Asian friend. She comes to the library several days a week and has really helped me communicate in basic Mandarin. I will miss her. I broke my promise to my brother and told her of our plan to go to London and eventually Hong Kong. She always asks me about my relation to Joko, and I tell her the truth. He must love me, but my family doesn't want me to get involved with anyone local. Tomorrow is my last day at the library, and I must explain and say good-bye to all the library employees. They have been so nice and helpful. Yet, I want to leave studying every day and use what I have learned. We tell everyone that we are moving to Constanta, the port on the Black Sea. My father's family lives there. Oh, I'm getting nervous! I have never been nervous! As soon as I go, I will be in someone else's hands. What if they are mean or uncaring? I just can't sleep; I'm too excited and worried. I won't even say good-bye to Joko. He will realize I'm gone and hear that our family moved to Constanta. I just know that he will try to follow me there. We will all drop off the face of the earth into new lives, new places, and in new roles. Now I had better get some rest. I have a long road ahead of me.

CHAPTER 39

WHAT A WAY TO HAVE SEX

I have not been able to sleep well. I really don't know how Constantin is going to get me a job in a luxurious five-star hotel as a maid. He has told us that the lady who is supposed to train us for a few weeks and is going to instruct us about city life. Loana isn't at all concerned about her future trip to Hong Kong. She is still a dreamer and thinks everything is resolved magically. I have been studying English, and I'm very good.

I don't understand my brother lecturing me on how I'm going to retrieve a condom with sperm. Then I need to place it in ice, go to an empty store room, and lock myself in. The next part of the plan is for me to attempt to push the sperm into my vagina. That really worries me. I'm afraid of getting caught. I'm afraid that it won't work. How will they know what single billionaire will go to a hotel with his girlfriend or a prostitute? They expect me to retrieve the used condom. If he throws it into the garbage. Maybe he will flush it down the toilet? Too many ifs for me. I'm not the quiet, patient girl with no concerns. I'm sure there's an alternative way. My sisters and I are all virgins. Can a virgin insert an instrument with sperm into her vagina? I have read about the impregnation of a woman, and I can't imagine that this will work. Doesn't the girl's hymen have to be broken first? We need to consult with a doctor about this. Maybe we need to have it broken first? Do we need to have intercourse first? I'm confused! I wish there was another way to obtain success.

I have a strong sense that Constantin's friend has feelings for me. I only saw him at that hotel restaurant, but he couldn't take his eyes off me. When I looked at him, he immediately moved his eyes in a different direction. Maybe there is nothing there, but I had a special feeling about him too. It seemed to be a mutual feeling? Maybe I wanted him to have feelings for me? To be honest, he is really something, an incredible guy, and my sisters agree. According to everything I see, his family might be rich. My brother would get angry if he knew my thoughts; the guy is his best friend.

I really don't know why we need to look for a billionaire; why can't we just find a decent, normal, honest working man? Why can't we stay together, and why leave our parents behind? Should we let Loana go so far away, to China? Why did he send Mihaela to America? Why complicate everything? I did not agree to using a false passport. They obtained them, and now we are using the real Romanian ones. All those things were wasted time and unnecessary. I believe the simple things are safer and more predictable. We don't have to look for billionaires. When I'm in England, I'm going to tell him how I feel. My father keeps on telling me to quiet down, that Constantin is a genius, and not to contradict him. Well, that's my father's opinion. My mother is also against this whole plan, but she is always against everything involving change. After I get a job and save some money, I'm going to bring them to London. Our parents are the best in the world. If I make a good salary, I don't need Constantin's plan. I want normal things, not magic billionaires a la carte.

Morning came, and the new experience of flying was smooth and easy for both Loana and me. Bucharest is beautiful, and it is wonderful to see Constantin and Dimitru. We were all ready for the continuing flight to London.

CHAPTER 40

OUR CHICKS HAVE FLOWN

"**W**ell, Sophy, my lifetime wish is about to begin, or it just began. Mihaela is in America; I hope she is well."

"Yes, don't worry; she is very bright and will know how to handle herself. Daniela and Loana just arrived in Bucharest, and they promised to call us often on this phone they left for us."

"Sophy, I know you didn't think Constantin's plan would work, but it's working. Pinch me!"

"What?"

"Pinch me, I said! I need to be sure that I'm not dreaming. Our dream of getting out of this slum has begun."

"Matei, explain how they are going to get these billionaires."

"Well, I don't really understand. Too complicated for me, but Constantin knows what to do. I trust him. This new friend, Dimitru, is helping him, and he has money to help. I liked him. How about you?"

"Well, he couldn't stop staring at Daniela. I'm afraid we might have a problem with him."

"Don't be silly, Sophy. He is a real friend. He gave Constantin over thirty thousand euros and rented an apartment in London. Constantin said he will lend him as much as necessary to make his plan work."

"I don't know. The girls will pay him when they are rich. Do you think they will take us out of here?"

"Well, you are still a beautiful woman, and many of these drinking men look at you with desire. and so do I. I will not take a chance. I hope that someday I can go out on the street without a weapon. I hate violence, but many times I have had to defend my children, my shop, and myself."

"Matei, I love you! Don't let them send Loana to China."

"But she is the one that wants to go. Well, we will see. The family plan has started."

LONDON, HERE WE ARE!

Constantin stepped out of the front door of the Uber followed by Loana, Daniela and Dimitru from the back. Only two suitcases and 4 beaming smiles, to enter the rented apartment in London. The landlady gave them their keys, and since it was a monthly rental, she insisted on taking pictures of all the furniture. She said that when they decide to move, she will take new pictures and compare them. "If you damage my furniture, you will pay, so keep things in order." Dimitru had guaranteed payment and damages. He used his credit card and reassured her that all would be in excellent order as it was now.

When the door shut, the girls looked at each other, and Daniela said, "Are we really here? Wow, this is amazing! What a trip—airports, airplanes, automobiles, traffic! We are really going to do this."

They proceeded to unpack the few items they had and tried to decide where each would sleep. As they were looking around the apartment, they heard the doorbell ring. Who could it be? No one knew them in London. Dimitru opened the door and found Mrs. French with a bunch of beautiful flowers and a plastic flower vase. She introduced herself as Mrs. Green. She told them she had decided to use her maiden name again. She seemed to be a sophisticated woman of about fifty but was very well cared for. She was warm and had a gentle way about her. She gestured with her hands when she spoke and emphasized her words with motion.

As they spoke with her, the question arose from Dimitru about which name she preferred. She said Mrs. Green. When asked why, she responded that she had recently discovered facts about her last husband. He had passed away recently. She found out he had a second home and children while he was married to her. She wanted to forget his name, feeling that he was such a shameful man. Mrs. Green was definitely an open and outgoing lady, very keen in her responses to all questions. Constantin nodded in approval to Dimitru. He understood that she was the right person to westernize his sisters. All agreed, and they made a series of plans for the next two weeks. The objective was to teach them a better grasp of English and to show them London and how to function as a Brit.

All of them enjoyed her conversation, and she left shortly after. They proceeded to take her advice and shop for food at a nearby market. Daniela murmured to Loana about how incredible everything was. What was ordinary and usual in London was very unique from their experience. They could tell that wonderful things were ahead. They simply had never been in a cosmopolitan apartment house, and everything was amazing to them.

Dimitru's gaze was always on Daniela. He was afraid everyone noticed. But he couldn't help it; he was mesmerized by her.

"So," Dimitru announced, "today is a very special day. I invite you to a great restaurant that I once went to with my parents. Let's put the shopping bags in the apartment."

Constantin reminded his friend that all the sisters had was what they were wearing and one change of clothes. Dimitru told them that Mrs. Green would definitely take care of that. He decided to postpone the special restaurant and instead introduced them to their first fast-food experience at McDonald's. He warned them that it was junk food and not to eat it often, but it was there when they were pressured for time. Daniela felt Dimitru's continued staring, and she stared back. She apparently liked what she saw and felt very warm feelings around him. Different from what she had ever felt before for a man. She thought, "What a different world."

CHAPTER 42

WHERE DID SHE DISAPPEAR TO?

J oko waited for the girls to leave the library. They always left at five thirty, just when his workday ended. Today something happened; they were not there. He traveled home and went to her father's shop, where he saw her parents in the shop together. That was really unusual. Where were the two girls? He'd already heard that Mihaela was in Constanta with her father's family. Later he went to the hill near their house. No one was there; the house was dark. He could always see one of them through the only window the shack had. Something strange was happening.

The next day, he skipped work and saw her parents walking to their shop. The girls were not around, no bus to the library. He then went to the library and spoke to the receptionist who always greeted Loana with a hug. "Hi, I'm looking for Loana and Daniela."

I'm sorry, but they are no longer here, and we don't expect them back.

He left and went to his house. Now he needed to figure out how he would he find his love. His mood became very dark and down. It was evening, and his father was at home after he had closed his accounting office for the day. His father's success allowed them to live in a middle-class neighborhood. His older brother was studying medicine at an American university. His father wanted Joko to study mechanical engineering, but Joko fell in love with this local girl. He refused to leave the town. Therefore, he studied mechanics. It was second best, but autos fascinated him.

Nothing was as enchanting as his Loana. He had barely spoken to her, yet he knew that she must be his life partner. His father noticed his mood and asked him about it. He couldn't explain that he loved a girl he barely knew, so he said, "Nothing is wrong!" He went to his computer and searched for the last name Woods in Constanta. Then, on second thought, he realized that they must be poor like Loana's parents and wouldn't have Internet presence. He became very angry and did something very unusual for him. He drank himself to sleep.

Joko could not believe the disappearance of Loana and her sisters. He followed their parents, but they were inseparable and in a routine that never changed. He didn't even have a phone number for Loana since she did not own a phone. Joko couldn't find her through that media. The thought of flying into Constanta to find the father's family came to mind, but it was a city of over two hundred and ninety thousand people. It was full of tourists enjoying the Black Sea beaches. Joko remembered that his parents took him there many times before. Also, the Woods were Gypsies and probably lived in slum areas, with no official ID papers. Was this a dead end? Joko was relentless and intelligent and he decided to return to the library and talk to some of the staff to see if there were any other clues to be found. First thing the next Monday morning, Joko appeared with several boxes of chocolate to see if he could buy, trade, or steal information about her whereabouts. His idea was to dress differently and elegantly, without the mechanic dungarees that he was usually seen in. Carefully he went from one staff member to the other, and almost all said the same thing after receiving the chocolate bribe. They all said to their best knowledge Loana and her family had gone to Constanta.

Joko started to leave in frustration, when suddenly he remembered the Asian woman that Loana always studied with. He returned and started to ask about the lady with the Asian background. There were very few people with Asiatic facial characteristics in our city. I hit the jackpot with the head librarian, who mentioned that the woman came every Friday to teach a children's class. Today was Monday, and they did not have and were not permitted to give him her name or address. That meant that he had to wait until Friday. Joko was highly frustrated and inpatient. He had to find Loana before Friday. What if she was off to marry someone else! Then, he suddenly thought that if the Asian woman lives in

Bistriţa, maybe the mayor's office or police department could help him. How many Asians live here? I had only seen them in Constanta and very few in Bucharest but none here in Bistriţa. I'll search. I need to find her, and I will not give up on my Loana.

CHAPTER 43

MIHAELA GOES BACK TO GO FORWARD

T he flight out of Washington DC was very relaxing; in fact I fell asleep right after the meal was served. I was lucky not to have any passengers in the two other seats. Then in Vienna, I was met by the lieutenant, who had already become a friendly face. He told me that he had arrived on an earlier flight, and was instructed to continue with me and to prepare me for the delegation meeting. He would explain how I should behave in the presence of the other participants. This was a part of the international cooperation that governments engage in, at the request of the host. The United States was invited to "help" with this assignment for the benefit of both countries. The lieutenant was definitely with the agency and spoke with authority.

He knew everything I had done in Washington. I had a kind of strange feeling that every action I had taken was recorded somewhere, and people were watching me. I'm just Mihaela, a small-town girl; how did I get to be so important that the US government cared about what I did, where I went, and who I spoke to? He proceeded to teach me how to use the small handheld computer that I was given. He also told me that I should not communicate with my family on my phone. The lieutenant deleted the WhatsApp. He told me I could call my family from the hotel phone.

This was the US plan, but I also had Constantin's plan to consider. I had intentions of seeing my brother and sisters before their trip to London the next day. He told me I would be too busy. If I wasn't worried before that, I was now!

"In two weeks when you return to Washington, you can call them, but you can't talk about your mission."

Mission. Now this had turned into a mission. I guess I am a spy.

He said, "I suggest you don't communicate with them. However, you can call your father from the hotel and tell him to tell the rest of your family that you are well. Your parents don't need to know about your mission either."

Mihaela, little by little, understood that she had just accepted to spy for the United States. Spies don't talk about where they are or what they do. All this was overwhelming! Yes, I accepted the job, with an incredible, beyond-belief salary that I could use immediately to get my parents out of poverty. I also knew that in five years' time, after I became a US citizen, I could ask for my parents' legal migration to the US. With all these positive things happening, I didn't have to follow Constantin's plan to blackmail a billionaire using his sperm. The idea of following the "billionaire thing" horrified me, and I secretly told my sisters. I shared that I was going to do whatever I could to get out of it.

Since I arrived from Austria, my first stopover point, my passport was not stamped. The entrance stamp was only necessary for direct flights from out of Europe or visa-requiring countries. I imagine that was one of the reasons why the lieutenant was assigned to be with me, to make sure my passport wasn't stamped. My trip to Teheran could not have evidence of foreign travel.

I was registered into a hotel near the embassy and told to relax and that I would be met by a Miss Sandersky, who would have lunch with me and continue giving me instructions for the assignment. Miss Sandersky was a tall woman who spoke in English with a Slavic accent, but she didn't speak Romanian, so we continued in English. She was to give me an intense course about how a magazine reporter acts, what the kind of information I must know and how to answer. She also gave me several copies of the *Petroleum Digest*, where I was supposed to be employed. Amazingly, it had my name printed inside as a field reporter. The magazine had started to function two months ago, and it included news about the industry and some advertising from restaurants and hotels. It looked real! I was told to memorize the names and nicknames of my colleagues on the desk of the magazine. In addition, I was given credentials and a CV. This reflected information about my "past."

Then they took my phone and installed a different chip so that I had a Romanian telephone number. She told me to paste the original chip into my US ID with tape and place it in an envelope. Finally, she accompanied me to the bank where a security box had been opened in my name. She placed these items identifying me as being connected to America into the box. Now I had absolutely no evidence of US ties.

An hour later I was taken to the petroleum building, ROPEPCA, on Tudor Stefan Street. Here I was to meet Katherina, my liaison with the Romanian delegation. I met her, and we immediately connected. We both had a common purpose, and it was at this point that all the arrangements for my trip were disclosed. I would be the only woman in the delegation. It consisted principally of Petroleum engineers, all but one of whom were Romanian. The non-Romanian was a Venezuelan. He had recently gotten a job after leaving his strife-ridden country. We were to have breakfast the next day and be ready for that evening. There was a KLM flight to Amsterdam as a stopover before arriving in Tehran. We would be met by a Romanian-speaking Iranian guide in Teheran. Katherina then asked me to come shop with her for some adequate clothing. The clothes needed to conform to the Islamic fundamentalist style of women's attire. All these new people, all these spies, and all these new clothes. Could this really be happening, or was this a dream? Would Mom come and wake me up in a few minutes? This is the stuff my books were filled with in the library—this could not be my life!

CHAPTER 44

MRS. GREEN, GUIDE TO THE NEW WORLD

Mrs. Green was interested in doing a fabulous job with these girls. Her son was an employee in charge of operations for Mr. Agnelli's Romanian oil concern. She had always wanted to help her son in something, and now for the first time, she had a chance to make him feel proud of her. She was retired from teaching English Literature at Brunel University. She had lots of experience with young women and their needs. She also knew how to instruct young women in correct manners. Both of the girls were dolls.

I don't know the real motive for them hiring me. Mr. Agnelli's son did mention employment, specifically in the finest hotels in London. Both young women were strikingly beautiful and seemed quite cooperative. There is nothing like a ready, willing, and able student. I was told that they were Romanian high-school graduates. They are very deficient in English and in proper manners. I thought that my work would be difficult. I didn't realize how thirsty they would be for what I had to impart to them.

I can't imagine what type of employment I can prepare them for. I'll start with grammar, proper writing, and pronunciation. Then they want me to help with dressing properly and makeup. This is to be a total makeover from both the physical, the intellectual and including the social graces. One of my second husband's sons was general manager of a boutique hotel, so maybe he can advise them. I'm sure they can work as receptionists or in the office. The only other job a hotel offers and always needs are maids. I don't imagine they want to do that. My impression is that they are willing to do whatever it takes to learn. Since they are with Mr. Agnelli's son, and I understand the family hit the lottery, I'm sure they have no economic problems and don't want menial jobs.

I received an envelope with twenty-five hundred pounds so they can purchase appropriate, sophisticated clothing. That is a lot of money, so that tells me that they are not needy. I also need to teach them how to use English money, how to bank, and how to get around the city, the country, and the world. Perhaps they could work in accounting in the hotel. My first step should be to check with my stepson before I make the offer. He is single, and I know that if he gets a look at them, along with my recommendation, they will be hired.

CHAPTER 45

A MOTHER WILL BE A MOTHER

Another protective mom was busy at work back in Bucharest. Dimitru was very close to us, his parents, and as an only child, it was normal for them to overprotect him. His mom wasn't too convinced Daniela was going to be what he said she was. He had shared a very dreamy impression saying, "I'm one hundred percent sure she is the woman of my dreams."

He is not only handsome, but he's very bright and has a wealthy future. Besides, he is my son, and I need to see if I can intervene in that final "dream woman" selection. I know she is pretty, but she comes from a Gypsy family. The family background definitely makes us edgy; we know that she must carry negative values. They say that stereotypes are not true, but what if they are, and there is negativity in this young woman? Those values would eventually be reflected in our grandchildren, if they married. My husband and I have been thinking of making an attempt to introduce him to someone my aunt Theresa recommended. Next week my aunt is arriving in Southampton, England, from New York on a cruise. She is traveling with her late husband's niece, Isabella. My aunt says she is gorgeous and is starting to study psychology at Columbia University. My thought was to ask Dimitru to please pick her up and invite her to our favorite fish restaurant, Randall & Aubin, in Soho. I already spoke to my aunt last week, and she has an idea of why I want to introduce him to Isabella. After that, we will let nature take its course.

CHAPTER 46

TOTALLY ON MY OWN

M ihaela thought, "I was so high fashion for such a short
time."I went shopping for long black dresses and black
head scarves and was advised to cut my nails short and
avoid using the eye makeup. The objective was to show no
sign of sexuality. Little did anyone know, I had just begun
with feminine adornments. I really liked it, and here I was going back to being the plain, nondescript girl that I was. I was
also advised not to talk unless spoken to. This seemed like it
was Dad telling us not to interact with our schoolmates or
the townspeople. I was told not to leave the hotel unaccom-
panied. Never take initiative; have the male engineers in the
delegation ask questions for me. All these restrictions were
expected from non-Muslim female foreigners. This seemed
easy enough; all I had to do was work behind the scenes and
"listen."

I paid for all my purchases with my debit card, and I was
taken to my hotel. There I was again met by my friend, the

lieutenant, and he placed an app on my iPhone and explained the following: "If you think a conversation in English, Farsi, or Arabic is interesting, please record it by touching app number one. If you need to take a picture of something interesting, try to do so without being seen. Then push button number two; this app will totally erase all the things you sent and leave no trace at all. This sounded easy enough, yet for the first time, I started to worry.

"Don't worry!"

"What should I consider interesting? I have not been trained."

"Don't worry; everything in Iran is interesting. We have very little information about what has been happening there for years. The reason you are being sent is that we have no one else with your talent. You are a Romanian in a Romanian scientific delegation that speaks English, Farsi, and Arabic. That's why we have been in such a hurry. Believe me; Iranians are very secretive and don't trust foreigners. With Romanians, they have no fear and might open up. Be careful, but don't worry, you have no US contact or any possible traceable history. You are a new amateur Romanian with no work experience being sent with the delegation. Zero suspicion!"

"What do I do with the laptop?"

"Well, you are a reporter, so write reports in Romanian to be sent later. Remember what I explained to you: there is little or no Wi-Fi anywhere in Iran. You, however, have this special phone that sends from anywhere without Wi-Fi. You have proven to us that you have common sense, and that's all you need. I was told in Washington to communicate daily with you. Yes, if you have nothing to inform us about, press button one or two, we will then know that there is nothing to report."

Mihaela asked, "how will I let my family know that I am well?"

"I'm sorry, but for the next two weeks, that is not possible."

He gave her a hug and left on that serious note. Mihaela thought of her quiet days in the library when she longed for adventure and excitement. Oh, to be back there now!

CHAPTER 47

A BILLION DOLLAR DEVICE

Back in Bistrita exciting changes were taking place. Joko decided to change his image. Everyone knew him as a mechanic in a small foreign-car shop. It's true, he was. But his area of expertise was the new electronics of engines. He decided not to go to a university in the United States, like his older brother, because he was focused on Loana. As an alternative he took several courses using his computer and the internet. The first courses were supported by Ashworth College. Next was a course from Oxford University. Following this he had completed programs from MIT and Georgia Tech. Although he was not an electronic engineer, he had hands-on experience with car engines. Being alone most evenings, he had developed a fuel processing technology app.

This app saved 60 percent of fuel consumption. It accomplished this by continuously fine tuning electronic engine performance. This revelation was his secret, and he kept this to himself. He only discussed it with his father, who believed in him but did not understand the simple complexity of the invention. His father was an accountant and did not fathom the enormity of his son's invention. Joko's big decision was whether to attempt to sell the invention to big auto-producing countries such as Germany, Italy, Japan, Korea, and China, who would want to bid to be the first to have his invention. An alternative would be to create a corporation in the United States and license the use of the app. All these aspirations included a great degree of danger and know-how that he did not have. Could he go to Silicon Valley and go into business with the aid of angel investors? He knew he had an immense moneymaker.

But Loana was on his mind. That night he asked for his father's Zolpidem pill. No other way to fall asleep. He definitely did not want to drink himself to sleep again. There was also the element of danger, which worried him. The oil companies would want to stop him in his tracks. Others would want to steal the invention and call it their own. Sleep, even with the pill, was rough. He drifted off thinking of being rich enough to hire professionals to trace Loana down and finally being able to marry her. Little did he know that she was in London exploring an exciting new life.

A NEW WORLD OUT THERE

This was going to be a very important day for the girls in London. It was "learning in life." Situations and behaviors had to be experienced to be addressed for the appropriate response. Mrs. Green intended to expose the girls to life as they would now know it. What a difference from their past. Each experience was a learning experience. This involved technology, manners, and proper personal interactions.

They began by going out for croissants with coffee at a nearby bakery. Every request was to be prefixed with "please" and ended with "thank you," even to the level of helpers in a restaurant. Napkins were to be placed upon the lap whenever eating. Pocketbooks were to be under the napkin and held close at all times. Everything was a moment of instruction, and Mrs. Green was very good at this.

Mrs. Green took them first to a bank and helped them speak to the bank official. They were to be aloof yet attentive.

Their aim was to open an account with accompanying debit and credit cards. As instructed, they asked a number of questions until they understood the use, difference, and restrictions of these various financial instruments.

The next stop was a cell-phone shop, where they bought a special offer of two phones for the price of one. They then sat down at the store for an hour of training. The training was twofold. They were learning the technical aspects as well as how to interact with the young salesman, who was immediately taken with them. It was time to put some early subtle flirting skills to use. After an hour they left the store, and the young man needed a coffee break to cool down. They picked up their new phones and started experimenting with all the different apps. In conclusion they left with gratitude for excellent customer service. Since male salespeople were involved, they got an even better price than normal, or so Mrs. Green commented. They began to realize the utility of their sexuality.

Following that she took them on a bus trip around the city to point out the different landmarks. They took note of the different ways of traveling around the city. She pointed out Buckingham Palace and the Parliament building and came close to 10 Downing Street, the prime minister's headquarters. Continuing on to Big Ben, they went by the Thames River and Trafalgar Square. It was getting late, and they stopped at Garfunkel's for a late lunch. They practiced the correct form and manners at the table and how to order and tip when service was adequate. They were very interested and internalized all the instructions. There would be no need to repeat the information.

It was a pleasure to have such attentive and bright students. They were smart young women, and they were getting smarter in the ways of the world day by day. Since we were not too far from the boutique hotel where Mrs. Green knew the manager, we walked by, and the students were impressed with the lobby. It was luxurious, and they appreciated the view. The manager was not in, so she told the receptionist to tell him that Mrs. Green had been there and that she would return with an appointment. She then called Dimitru to let him know we had finished for the day. The next day was to be rainy, so we would dedicate our day to conversation and grammar. They thanked Mrs. Green properly and joined their brother and friend to continue their amazing exploration of London. They had a lot to learn, but they were ready and highly receptive. This was only their first day out and about, and wonderful things were ahead for them, they could just tell.

CHAPTER 49

BEAUTY COMES IN THREE

"Constantin, I'm going to be busy today on a private matter for my mother," Dimitru said. "Since your sisters are being tutored, why don't you relax, and I'll let you know if I am free later?" "OK" Dimitru took his rented car and drove to the Southampton Port. There his aunt Theresa was going to arrive on a Royal Caribbean cruise ship from New York. She planned to stay in London for a while.

My mother asked me to pick my aunt up, take her to her hotel, and invite her for dinner. My mom knows that I do not like to do things like this, but my aunt is an older lady, and Mom insisted. I am surprised she decided to travel alone. She has mobility issues; however, she is very clever and has been a widow for a long time. I guess that she wanted to travel while she still can. I can't blame her.

My situation in the apartment is both dramatically wonderful and terrible at the same time. I see Daniela, and I melt. She is royalty in my eyes. When she talks I feel she is the smartest and sweetest person ever. Now, for the first time in my life, I'm convinced that I'm in love, real love. She is right there, and I haven't even touched her. How frustrating—just her closeness excites all my neurons and gives me tachycardia. I don't know how to act in front of her. I'm 100 percent sure that Constantin is aware—he knows me well—but when I'm near Daniela, he might perceive my heart fluttering. He is also a man, although he never talked of having been in love. Maybe his extremely sheltered life did not permit him to meet someone? Now he is just all about "the plan"!

But in Bucharest at the institute, he had an affair or two. It struck me that Constantin hadn't explained the details of his plan, specifically how his sisters were going to meet these very wealthy men, the billionaires. I don't understand his talk about them getting jobs as hotel maids. Maybe that's how Gypsies think? My friend Constantin, in just two years, has become a man of the world. He is as good a student as I am, in everything both academic and worldly. I have been thinking of asking to establish a company with him as my partner. That would be easy, but how do I tell him that I'm in love with his sister? I know that Daniela knows or feels my emotions are caused by her. She seems to like my silent advances. For a country girl, she picked up the unspoken messages, and I believe that she was receptive. It is the next steps that I am worried about. Will she accept my overt advances? Will she reject me for "the plan?" How will Constantin take the news?

When I arrived my aunt was already on land. She had finished her immigration and customs requirements. From afar

I could see she was accompanied by a nurse or helper. I didn't realize that she would be using a wheelchair. I hugged her, as I hadn't seen her for a few years, and my mother had recently been flying to New York to meet with her frequently. This was her only remaining sister. Now I understood the urgency of going to see her so often. Her health was failing, and each time might be the last. Her assistant was introduced as her late husband's niece, and her name was Isabella. I took a fast glimpse at her, and wow! She was something special. My God! I'm surrounded by extremely beautiful women. What's happening? But "Daniela is my future; Daniela is my life" is what went through my mind. My aunt insisted that Isabella sit up front, and for the next half hour, all she did was talk about Isabella—her intelligence and her abilities.

It didn't take me long to understand my mother also had a plan. She apparently wasn't convinced that Daniela was for me, so she planned Isabella's encounter with me. I know how my parents think. I dropped my aunt and Isabella off at the hotel and invited them for dinner as instructed by my mother. I also added that I had some friends in London who would be joining us. I then called Constantin and invited him and his sisters to a very special restaurant with my aunt and her niece. I was very well aware that in the restaurant our table would be the center of attention for every man within viewing distance of these three beautiful women. I was interested to see Constantin and his sisters' response to Isabella.

CHAPTER 50

THE CALL THAT FINALLY CAME

Matei and Sophy were still in Bistrita waiting for news of their children' exploits. In Matei's home the cell phone finally rang. He picked it up clumsily and answered, not being used to talking into this little box. In the neighborhood only the tough kids had cell phones. Often it was acquired by stealing it.

Mihaela was on the phone. She said she was well and had gotten a good-paying job in America. Soon she would call again, but now she was in a hurry. "Call Constantin, and tell him I'm OK and that I will call him in two weeks."

"Two weeks? Couldn't she call sooner? That is a very long time not to hear from her. Even so this call made me so happy." Immediately after her call, he attempted to call Constantin, but there was no answer, or had the call not gone through? He probably forgot what he was supposed to touch first before touching numbers; these things were very confusing, and Sophy was even afraid to hold this gadget. He knew that in a very short time, maybe a few months away, he would be told to sell or give away their things and move to where their children lived. They were happy the plan has started working.

"There is this boy, who keeps coming by the shop. He only hangs out nearby but doesn't come in. He must be looking for one of our daughters. Oh! We sure all the young men were always trying to meet up with them. We understand; we were young once. They say it's the hormones that are active at that age—whatever! I'm sure in a short time, he will give up and stop passing by. He must realize they are gone. If he comes in and asks, we have our answer ready. They are in Constanta, and they are living with their family, no phones, no numbers—gone."

CHAPTER 51

THE UNDERSIDE OF THE PLAN

When Dimitru informed me that he was busy with a family matter, I decided to go to the Westminster Reference Library. I was there to do some research. I had found out that I could sit in the library and use the reference section without signing in. That meant that I was leaving no paper trail. I could do the research that I needed to make the geographic and logistic connections with the super wealthy. The first thing I did was review *Forbes Billionaire Special Edition* from the last two years. Wow, I found a gold mine! London and New York were an oasis for the superrich, and Hong Kong was not far behind. I didn't need any more sources; I had more than I could handle. I started to make my listings of the older men, and I researched their children and grandchildren. I took paper notes and photocopied a trove of information. I calculated that I'd need a few weeks to get my data organized. I was able to use the library's public-access computers without divulging my name or information. On the Internet, I saw that some of them owned hotels and spas everywhere in the world, including London. I started writing down hotels to visit for job applications for the girls.

I was so enthusiastic. My plan was advancing impressively, smoothly, and expediently. My sisters would be proud of the incredible progress I had made in just a few hours. I had bought a UK telephone chip with Dimitru and wanted to call my parents, but Dimitru called to invite us to a special restaurant for that evening. This dinner sounded important to Dimitru, and I could not say no. I could never say no to Dimitru after all he had done and was doing for myself and my family. Knowing that I had to make a proper impression, I went to a men's shop and bought myself a jacket and tie for the special occasion. I then called one of my sisters' phones to tell them to be ready at seven o'clock. Since it was still afternoon and they were with Mrs. Green, I told them to ask her to prep them for a formal dinner out. This would be an evening with elegant company.

Following this flurry of activity, I did call my father, and he was so happy because he had attempted to call but had forgotten how to use the phone in WhatsApp. I had to be patient and walk him through the process again. As I spoke he used Mom's phone to perfect his understanding. He was a hands-on kind of person. Anyway, he told me of Mihaela's very brief call and understood that she was not able to talk freely. I too was worried and thought that two weeks was a long time, but there was nothing I could do but wait.

I prepared for this wonderful dinner with Dimitru's family, and I thought again about withholding from Dimitru my real plan's details regarding my sisters. He had hinted at not understanding, but each time I changed the subject. I knew he would not agree because in his non-Gypsy world, he wouldn't understand how terrible a life we had led. We were ready to go to extremes to get out forever from that life. I'm sure that my sisters aren't too happy with my plan; they also want to fall in love and marry like my parents and have children by choice and not by force with some unknown sperm and a pipette. No love, no contact, no warmth—cold, calculated infusion. I feel sorry for their part of this ordeal. They will have to deal with denial, lawyers' insults, and possibly judges. The money will come, but at a price. Do we have a choice? As simple employees somewhere, where are we going to be? I also need love; I have never been in love. I have never felt that feeling that I see in movies and the books I read. Hopefully, after my plan is complete and my sisters are set for a good life, I will be lucky to find someone to really love. My friend Dimitru has been acting really strange but only when he is around Daniela. I sometimes think he has feelings for her. She is beautiful and bright—why wouldn't he be taken with her? He insists that I'm so excited that I'm seeing things that don't exist. She has been so overwhelmed the last few weeks that it's hard to tell if Daniela has similar feelings. We are all so close, being involved with all these changes. Time will tell, but I need to keep a careful eye out since I have taken on this family responsibility

CHAPTER 52

THE OLDEST PROFESSION

Since Constantin had unscheduled time he decided to visit one of the hotels that catered to billionaires he had read about. Once there, he sat down in the coffee shop to observe the movement of guests and their physical characteristics. After his second coffee, a young woman sat near his booth. She placed herself in a strategic position as if waiting for someone.

She was tall and very pretty and, I might add, very nervous. Every time the hotel door opened, she immediately reached out to see if it was the person she was expecting. Finally, an older man came in and went straight to the reception desk. A minute later she received a phone call, and I concluded it was from the person who had come in. She waved to him, and he approached her and sat down right behind me. They exchanged a few words, and then she excused herself and went to the ladies' room. What really happened, as I observed from my booth, is that she hurriedly left the hotel. I assumed she didn't like the looks of the older gentleman. He waited patiently, and after twenty minutes and several phone call attempts, I decided to talk to him.

"Excuse me," I said.

He looked at me with a grin.

Constantin said, "Evidently, the one that was going to meet me never even showed up."

He then asked me if I would join him at his table, and I did. He ordered a drink, and I decided to have my third coffee. He started asking me questions about my nationality, my accent, and my profession. I made up a story about being a son of a very wealthy Romanian family and coming to London for some fun. After his second drink, he gave me his card, and it was impressive. He was a baron, and principal proprietor of a British worldwide shipping concern. He went into a long story about his wealth and how unhappy the passing of his third wife had left him. He needed company and had arranged a well-known escort agency to supply him with someone tall and beautiful, but she apparently didn't like his looks, and she spoke only Hungarian. "She must be a newcomer," he said. He went on to say that he had prepaid over five hundred pounds for a few hours with her. He asked me which agency I had called, and I didn't want to involve myself into more false stories, so I told him it was a gorgeous waitress I met in a restaurant. He went on to tell me that London, and most cities in Europe, were full of women for hire. He also went on to tell me that one of the women he had been with had attempted to save his sperm, most likely with bad intentions. He advised me to be careful. "All these women are after our money. The rich have to be careful."

The baron paid and then excused himself to go to the bathroom. As I got up to leave, right in front of me, I bumped into Ann. She was the young woman I had helped on my first trip to London. She had seen me and had come up to greet me. We sat down, and then I saw the baron wink at me and shout out, "Good choice!" as he went to the hotel exit.

Ann was dressed well, but she was there to meet a client. I decided that I was not going to try to save her from herself. She was evidently a lost case.

CHAPTER 53

A TABLE FOR 6 AND INFATUATION FOR 4

D imitru decided to keep his rented vehicle for the evening to be able to pick up and deliver his aunt and make her accessibility easier. He went back to his apartment, and Loana was watching TV. This had become a way of learning language and culture at the same time as relaxing—what a treat. The family was relaxed, even though Dimitru was there, as he had become one of them. Daniela was taking a shower. She was tired after a complete day of grammar and literature from their tutor. Loana called into Daniela to hurry up because she was next in the shower, and then it was Dimitru's turn. Time to get ready was running short.

Rushing, Daniela came out with a towel around her gorgeous body. Dimitru started to breathe heavily. He moved away, afraid to show his reactive emotion. They were alone for the first time, and she definitely perceived his interest and excitement. But it was not one-sided; she looked into his eyes with a similar feeling and desire. This was too much for anyone to restrain. He started to move toward her, and she did not move. There was complete silence; a pin drop would have been heard. Loana's shower running was all they heard, along with the TV in the background. He continued to approach her, and she looked at him with emotion and maybe fear. Their lips met briefly, and he told her, "*Te iubesc asa de mult.*" She nodded as if to say she knew and she also felt it. She then moved closer to him with a light peck on his lips.

Their excitement was suddenly interrupted by the sound of keys outside the apartment. Daniela suddenly went into her room. Thirty seconds later Constantin came into the apartment with a very happy grin, after an excellent day. He started to tell Dimitru all about his billionaire search. A few minutes later, Loana shouted to Dimitru that she had finished, and it was his turn to shower.

He showered with very cold water. He had an indescribable mix of conflicting emotions. He was definitely in love and was so happy that she knew and had responded affirmatively. Now they both had a secret. Was it easier this way, or harder? They wanted to be together, but both were afraid of the consequences. Him from his best friend, she from her family and their goals for her. He just ruined Constantin's plan, but he was ready to begin his own plan. The thoughts flooded in as the water flooded down. A moment to remember, a turning point in life, it was all becoming clear to him now. His life was beginning, along with theirs and involved with theirs.

Dimitru left first so he could pick up his aunt and Isabella with the car. The others went to the restaurant using the underground subway. Daniela spoke to Loana and told her what happened, and they were both flabbergasted. But they knew for now silence was the only way to go. They both liked Dimitru and treasured his kindness and friendship to the family. Daniela loved him, she was sure.

They arrived before Dimitru, the table had been reserved, and Constantin explained all his findings of the day. Loana explained their day, and strangely Daniela was silent. She acted and looked distracted. When Isabella and the aunt arrived, everyone ordered a drink. They had been trained by Mrs. Green in how and what to order. When Constantin was introduced to Isabella, an incredible reaction presented itself. Constantin started to behave just like Dimitru when he was near Daniela. What do you call this instant immediate attraction? It was a mutual situation, as when Isabella and Constantin shook hands, neither he nor she let go. The aunt was incredulous and wanted to tell Isabella he was the wrong one. It was too late; something magical had happened.

Their table had the finest service from all the waiters in the restaurant. At one point even the chef came out to see if everything was to their liking. He had never done that before, but he heard stories of this one table and he had to come to see for himself. He reentered the kitchen saying nothing was exaggerated about the women at that table. Loana thoughts wandered to, *I wish that Mihaela was here to witness and experience all of this with us.*

CHAPTER 54

YOU CAN'T HIRE BEAUTY

Mihaela was having her own eye opening experiences thousands of miles away. Flying wasn't so new to her anymore. She enjoyed changing airlines so she could compare them in her mind. The Romanian delegation consisted of eleven men and one woman! All the men, young and old, came up to greet her personally. Her parents had always told her that she was beautiful, but they were her parents. Now she got the feeling that she really was special. They had been advised that a woman reporter would be with the delegation. When they saw her face, they were happy to see a young, attractive, smiling woman. They had no idea who she really was or what she was doing there. In addition they could not see the rest of her anatomy; it was covered in a long black dress. As they imagined, a veil or scarf would be in place as soon as they landed in Tehran.

Next to her sat Rafael, a thirty-year-old oil engineer who spoke some Romanian and fairly good English. He had been hired recently by one of the big oil firms in Bucharest. During the flight he told her that his specialty was modern drilling techniques He had developed a high-tech method. It was going to be useful for the company. He originally came from Venezuela, a nation with the largest oil reserves in the world, but right now they were in economic ruin. Therefore, he accepted the job in Romania. The real reason, he explained, was the extreme political strife and kidnappings that had his native country at a standstill. He needed to make a salary in dollars to help his parents, brothers, and sisters survive the harsh economic reality. She spoke to him in English because his Romanian was not well refined. He was a gentleman, unlike most Romanian men, who immediately measured your anatomical dimensions.

She knew he wasn't happy with this mission to accompany the delegation, but his company thought he knew enough to identify what in Iran could be useful for their firm. At thirty he was the youngest of the men and the only one with a US education. He was also afraid of the very distrustful Iranian fundamentalists he might encounter. Anyway, since they were the two youngest in the group, it was natural to hang out together.

After the arrival, they were dispatched by bus to a hotel, this one totally different from the Washington experience. It was an old, rundown, sad room with no evidence of maintenance or cleaning. The guide said it was the best that was available. After a quick late lunch, they were guided on a tour of Tehran. They were shown the Milad and Azadi Towers.

The Milad is Iran's tallest building, and they went up to the viewing deck. A 360-degree view of Tehran was visible. They were taken to Golestan Palace and visited a museum. They finished with the Sa'dabad Complex. The guide said it had unique architectural characteristics. They arrived back at the hotel restaurant for a light dinner. There was no menu choice. They ate what was presented in a small buffet. Since they didn't see any other guests in the dining room, they assumed the room was only for their group. The next day, they concluded that they were the only guests in the hotel.

Rafael and Mihaela gravitated to one another. Initially it seemed it was because of their English-speaking ability, but then it felt like his personal pattern of endearment, or was it she that became endeared to, or for, him? Now that she looked at him more carefully, he was strikingly handsome and apparently muscular which she liked. She didn't know what it was, but it didn't really matter? They were in Iran, a country ruled by a religious group that permitted no public display of intimacy, and this meant that she was not alone. She felt that she did have a certain power over men, even in these ultraconservative clothes. One by one all the delegates, married or not, sought her out for conversation. When she walked into the room, she was the center of attraction. She had even noticed the men in Tehran take a second take when they saw her, even through the veil. With them she felt danger; with Rafael she felt safe.

CHAPTER 55

THE ASIAN CONNECTION IS FOUND

J oko visited the mayor's office and the police department, but was not successful. He couldn't find the mysterious Asian library figure. He took advantage of his newfound free time to write to different companies and make inquiries. He reached out to possible investing firms in Silicon Valley. He wanted to test out the idea of the app he had perfected. His purpose was to see who realized the importance of his invention. He also went to the Bistriţa branch of the top patent law firm from Bucharest. He inquired about the procedure of patenting internationally. There were expenses involved. Would his dad front the money for an invention he did not understand? He already had an idea that through the Internet, the world of information, perhaps he could find less-expensive alternatives. Now he had two missions in life: finding his love and succeeding in business through his invention. His business was in the works with feelers out in all directions—now for his love. Passion motivated him! Joko was a man of action.

On Friday morning at nine o'clock, he patiently waited in the library for her to arrive. He was then told that her name was Mrs. Lee, and she was on time and very friendly. She told him she had seen him many times at the library and Loana was aware of his feelings toward her. Amazingly, Mrs. Lee said Loana had left a message for him. The content of the message read as follows: "I am sure that you will try to contact me. I also have feelings for you."

Mrs. Lee followed up with, "She told me to tell you that she is sorry she left without ever talking to you. She wanted to explain that her family had a plan for her to meet and marry a very wealthy man." Mrs. Lee continued to share. "Since she wanted to go to China, specifically Hong Kong, I taught her sufficient Mandarin for her to start a conversation. Loana was a fast learner."

"Where is she?" he asked.

"Her brother's friend from Bucharest is helping her. She went to Bucharest last week but then on to London, and finally to Hong Kong. I don't know the timetable. I'm sorry. I know you are in love with her; she assumed that."

"Yes, that's why I'm here."

Mrs. Lee continued. "I followed my instincts after falling in love with my friend, a Romanian student in Shanghai, and I searched and finally found him here in Bistriţa. We are married and now have two children. I am so happy for the two of you. You need to find her. She is a lovely girl. Don't give up." With that Mrs. Lee gave him her phone number and rushed to her library class.

His happiness was indescribable. He went directly to his father's office and interrupted him because he had something important to discuss. He had to fly to Bucharest to find Constantin's friend who would lead him to Loana. He gave his father a recap of the conversation with Mrs. Lee. Then he told his father he would resign from his job immediately and he needed a loan from him to pursue the woman of his dreams. Now he knew Loana felt the same way.

CHAPTER 56

CONSTANTIN'S ABRUPT DIVERSION

It was unbelievable. When Dimitru came into the restaurant with his aunt, I realized that behind him, carrying a bag, was a woman. I gazed at her face, at her eyes, and I couldn't take my eyes off of her. Dimitru introduced us to Isabella, and I grabbed her hand and couldn't let go. I was mesmerized! After a minute or so, which seemed an eternity, we released our hands, but not our eyes. We were fixed on each other. I immediately thought to myself, "I found her, before I even started to search for the love of my life." I started to sweat, had chills, and began shaking. I think I had difficulty breathing. It was an electric moment.

She finally said, "I'm so glad to meet you. Dimitru didn't stop talking about you."

Dimitru gave her a strange look. He later told me that he

had only mentioned me once or maybe twice. It was apparent that Isabella and I had fallen instantly in love. Daniela instinctively got up and gave Isabella her seat next to me. She sat right next to Dimitru.

I had a feeling that Dimitru had just resolved two problems, mine and his. What a change! What is happening to my plan? This might be better than my plan. But I still had Loana and Mihaela alone, and the plan would continue. If Dimitru is as serious as he looks, Daniela is his. I'm not going to oppose that. He is such an incredible person, and so are his parents—wonderful people. Will they accept my sister? I hope so. I'm starting to believe in God. He sent me Isabella, without warning and without any effort. When we sat next to each other, I automatically held her hand, and she was as happy as I was. Maybe after she finds out why I'm in London and about my zero wealth and zero future, she will change her surprising instant love encounter toward me.

"So, you're Isabella? And where are you from? Are you working, or are you related to Dimitru's aunt?"

She tried to answer; I don't know what she said. All I heard was my heart beating like crazy, and a part of me was astounded at what was happening. I didn't even notice that Daniela and Dimitru were also holding hands and locked in as sensual a gaze as I was with my newfound woman. Dimitru's aunt didn't talk. All she did was stare with disbelief. She evidently was totally surprised at what happened. That left my sister Loana with a confused grin.

She actually was the only sane person at the moment, and she responded to the waitress by ordering drinks and appetizers for the center of the table. She had learned from Mrs. Green.

CHAPTER 57

LOVE AND WEALTH ARE CLOSE AT HAND

That night, Joko slept without the need of sleep enhancement methods. The proof that Loana was going to be his was such incredible news. He felt like calling Mrs. Lee a hundred times to ask her for more information. What stopped him from calling was that he knew she had told him everything she knew. His father had given him his blessing on his decision and access to his credit cards for whatever he needed. He went to speak to his boss at the garage and explained the reasons for his leaving. The man loved Joko and his excellent work and told him that whenever he wants his job back, it's his. He proceeded to buy a ticket to Bucharest on the first flight on Monday. During the weekend he prepared and packed all the paperwork and testing evidence to prove the fuel consumption efficiency of his app system. He used his father's office equipment to make a video presentation, just in case he needed to explain his invention. His English was technically good but conversationally deficient. He continued to read and watch news and films in English. He had recently read F. Scott Fitzgerald's *The Great Gatsby*, and how appropriate was one of his statements: "His dream must have seemed so close that he could hardly fail to grasp it."

Now his happiness was so evident, one of his father's office associates stopped him and said, "You seem to be walking on air, and your eyes are glistening!"

He laughed and reassured him. "No, I never take drugs."

They both laughed loudly, and most of the office applauded his victorious feeling.

Monday morning, Joko searched his phone for new e-mails as he was on his way to the airport. It was a forty-minute drive, and he received another surprise—several responses to his interest inquiry letters about the app. The Wi-Fi in the area did not exist, so he could not open up the mail. The small local airport did not have Wi-Fi either. A little frustrating. In Bucharest, he checked into a small hotel and immediately checked his e-mail. To his surprise, Exxon, who he didn't write to, reached out, saying, "We are very interested, and if you agree we can have one of our high executives visit you in Romania." Ford and GM were also very interested in talking to him. They both offered first-class tickets to their main offices. Japan and German car manufacturers asked him to contact them before talking to anyone else.

My God. What happened? This is incredible, but the Loana search is my priority. I need to find her. Maybe she is in Bucharest. After jetting through the Internet for the name Constantin Wood and getting zero results, I started calling all the universities and technology institutions. All of them answered that they were not at liberty to give out student's information. I then decided to visit the University of Bucharest first. If I dressed like a rich person, with a vest, tie, and jacket, I might impress the secretary, who would give me the information. I'll go shopping and also buy a leather briefcase to heighten my status. I tried on a hat, but I honestly didn't look good, although the saleslady said that I would kill the ladies with my hat on.

At the university, my clothing must have made a difference. I was received by the dean of students, an interview usually difficult to obtain. He wasn't helpful at all. When I exited his office, his secretary slipped me a small note with her phone number. I called her after I left the building., and she told me that she felt that my quest was in vain and that she checked all the student listings and there were no students with Wood as their last name. She was a darling.

After visiting five institutions with no success, I returned to my hotel and decided to call a friend, really my father's friend, Mr. Gavidescu. He had helped my father go through very difficult moments when my mother was very ill and passed away. He invited me to his house, near Bordei and Floreasca Park, an excellent high-end neighborhood. He and his wife received me with joy. They were never able to have children but dedicated all their free time and wealth to helping foster homes and children's hospitals. They insisted I stay at their house, but I needed to have the freedom of movement and I didn't accept. After telling them my story, he told me that his business partner at their insurance company had once hired a detective to help him locate a nephew who had eloped and whose parents were in distress. The next day he would make his inquiry and call me with information.

I decided to tell him about my gasoline-saving app. He offered access to one of his friends, the owner of a very big Romanian petroleum company, the Agnelli Company. This Romanian company was present in many parts of the world, and he could give me proper advice. I thanked him, but I was interested in a big car manufacturer, not an oil company. The oil companies would try to stop my invention from being used, or so I suspected. He insisted that this man, Mr. Agnelli, was his best friend and would advise me honestly. He added, Mr Agnelli had also used that detective with success. My priority was finding Loana. Mr. Gavidescu understood. Joko's app would disrupt the price and need for oil on the world market. That fact would affect economies of oil producing nations.

STRANGE BEDFELLOWS

Secretly serving the US interests Mihaela spent the second day in Tehran.

They took us to a building for films about the history of the Iranian petroleum industry—a long and boring series of videos in English with Romanian subtitles. Petroleum was their main product and the lever of their political power then, an older speaker with an English accent addressed us. He said he had studied in London and that was where he had acquired an English accent. He began his talk by blasting the United States and the embargo against Iranian products. He stated that the treaty the West signed was due to their fear of the Iranian military and possible nuclear potential.

He continued by saying, "Now they gave us back our money, and we have started to rebuild our drilling and production capacity. We will be able to supply all of Europe and Asia." He wore a turban and a beard, and his language seemed menacing and very loud. I think he wanted us to fear him. I personally did not feel afraid; I had nothing to fear. I was the only woman in the conference room, and I was treated as if I were not there. Coffee was served to the men by male waiters. But my coffee was left on a side table. Men could not get near me, no less serve me, was my thought. We were given sufficient information about Islamic customs in this country.

The next step was lunch with Iranian oil engineers. Rafael sat next to me, and he seemed a little nervous when he saw the Iranians coming in. He excused himself and went to the men's room. He stayed in the bathroom for over half an hour. I became worried and told one of the Romanians to go into the bathroom to see what was wrong. By then most of the Iranians had left. The Iranian counterparts spoke to the men, but I was ignored. Everyone looked at me from afar but didn't even nod or acknowledge my existence. Rafael came out and excused himself. He ate hurriedly and told me he would explain later. I took notes at the lectures because that was expected of me, even though I did not understand all the technical material.

That evening, when we were having dinner, the head of the Romanian group asked us all to meet in an outside garden after the meal. We didn't know why he didn't say whatever he had on his mind there in the dining room. He put his finger on his mouth to shush us into silence. We went out to the garden obediently, and we were not followed. He led us to a corner and nervously told us that there were hidden microphones everywhere, even on the bus, in the bathroom, and in the dining room. Although we had no secrets, we should be careful. Romania was part of the West. It is a Christian and democratic country, but they always looked for propaganda victims. Therefore the less we talked the better. He said that he was totally bored and predicted that this trip was apparently useless. They were not going to show their installations. "Mihaela suggested that we ask them to show us other towns and attractions. If their plan was to keep on showing us videos every day, we will go crazy." They all agreed and laughed. We were told we couldn't leave the hotel because it was unsafe. There were no bars because alcohol was forbidden in Iran. The TV was in Farsi, with one Arabic station. No music, no movies—only news, all the time.

Rafael motioned for me to stay in the garden. The others left little by little. There was nothing to do but go to sleep early. Rafael found a corner that he calculated was out of sight from the hotel room windows, and whispered into my ear. "I need to talk to you in private. Can I come to your room?"

I looked at him and hesitated, but he seemed to be honest and a gentleman.

He said, "We can't talk, but we can write on paper and then flush the papers down the toilet."

I was worried about cameras in the halls or stairs. He said he would check to see if he could see any. I told him I was in room 277, and he said he was in 270. "If I feel safe, I'll come at nine o'clock." It was seven o'clock Tehran time.

He came at nine o'clock. They went into bathroom, and

she put on the shower so noise would be lessened. He wrote: I studied engineering at the University of Texas, and I saw someone who studied with me. He was a total bully. He had many unfortunate incidents with me during our studies. I was a summa cum laude graduate, and he didn't achieve that honor. He blamed me and even threatened to beat me up at that time. He is the really big Iranian that had lunch with our group. If he sees me, I'm in trouble.

She wrote: What's his name?

Hamid, he wrote.

"Now I understand," she murmured silently.

He evidently was very worried. He started to leave.

She wrote: Don't! You will be safer with me.

He made a hand expression asking, "How?"

She answered with a shrug. Then she wrote: I'm afraid for you.

They tore the papers up and flushed them down toilet. Then, owing to stress, time change, and sheer exhaustion, they both laid down in bed, both totally dressed, and after a while fell asleep. They forgot to stop the shower, until she awoke during the night and shut off the water. The first time she ever "slept" with a man. Different from what she expected. If only she could tell her sisters what a strange first sleeping experience she had with a man. He was handsome, bright, poor, and she had feelings for him. How did this fit into "the Plan"?

CHAPTER 59

LONDON'S PLAN IN JEOPARDY

Ioana was so happy. Her brother had instantly fallen in love with the most beautiful woman they both had ever seen.

Models in magazines that I have seen at the library were not even close. It made me think of that boy, Joko. I knew he had special feelings for me, and after a while, I started feeling the same way. I hope he went back to the library to ask about me; that will be the test. I left him a message with Mrs. Lee. I dreamed of him holding me and kissing me and being intimate with me. I hope he pursues me, but he is only a mechanic. He won't be able to help my family. Besides, it will ruin Constantin's plan. I'm in a dilemma. Should I follow my dream or go and get pregnant from an unknown billionaire?

Now it's Mihaela and I, since Daniela found her man and she is out of the plan. I saw Constantin so happy that Dimitru was with Daniela. How confusing all this is. I got up this morning and decided not to stay in London. I want to go and try my luck in Hong Kong. I'm going to talk to Constantin as soon as he returns. I don't know where he went, maybe to visit Isabella. Joko, please find me! I don't know his last name. I don't know where he works now, since I left. I don't know how to reach him. Maybe if I call Mrs. Lee we will find a way to be in touch. Life is really strange! This is not what I ever expected. Is Joko lost to me?

Meanwhile in Bucharest Mr. Gavidescu decided that Joko really needed help he seemed very lost. Early Tuesday morning he attempted to get the detective's telephone number for him. To accomplish that, he contacted Mr. Agnelli on his cell phone. There were two important topics. First, he needed the phone number of the detective he had employed in the past. Second, he talked to him about whatever he understood of the gasoline app. Sharing the requested phone number was easy, and he did so right away. Mr. Agnelli said he didn't know how to help him relating to his app, but if this was important, he'd meet him.

"I'm in Madrid right now. Ask him to come to my office on Friday at ten o'clock. I'll listen to the details and try to think of how to help."

"How are your wife and Dimitru?"

"My wife is with me, and Dimitru is in London with a friend. He is doing very well also."

As soon as he hung up, Mr. Gavidescu called Joko's phone and gave him all the information. He invited him to his house again and reassured him that the detective was very good and had many political connections, which would help with his quest to find Loana.

Joko's world was expanding in his international attempt to track his Loana.

CHAPTER 60

TWO MEN ONE WOMAN

Mihaela got up very early and reviewed all the things that happened. Sleeping next to her was Rafael, and he was sleeping soundly. She looked at his Latin features, noting his thick eyebrows and athletic frame, which was visible even though he was fully dressed. The fact that he didn't try to take advantage of her showed that he was sincere. It also demonstrated that he trusted her enough to come in her room when he was distressed.

He took this risk in a dangerous environment and stayed with me when I asked him to. Last night I felt so afraid, I even took the risk of being discovered. That helped me to decide that I needed to take action to help Rafael. There is a chance Hamid will recognize him. Hamid had been his opponent, and he beat Hamid for the honor of summa cum laude. This is the man that was the cause of Hamid's shame. I washed up and very quietly, woke him up, and wrote on a paper, "I am leaving. You leave after I leave, and I'll see you downstairs." I gave him a kiss on his cheek and left.

Just awakened Rafael thought: *my life has crossed a number of nations in a short time. I was born in Caracas, Venezuela, and I'm a petroleum engineer. I studied in the Central University of Venezuela first, and then I continued on at a two-year program at the University of Texas. There I studied modern drilling techniques. It was very useful for the government company where I worked, PDVSA. Since the government became socialist, all the oil in the country was government owned. My family historically has always been democratic, therefore I was soon treated as a second-class citizen. I was completely ignored even though I initiated all the changes for safer drilling. Instead of being promoted, I was demoted as the political situation suffered even more. There were continued kidnappings, food shortages, and medicine from unreliable countries or a total lack of certain medicines. The most competent, trained doctors were forced to leave the country. The medical system was insecure and lacked everything to perform proper treatment. My salary, which had been very good, became impossible to live on with the 1,200 percent devaluation that now exists. I applied for jobs outside of Venezuela and was offered jobs in Saudi Arabia, Kuwait, and Romania. I accepted this country because it was a democracy. I couldn't continue to live under fear and stress. I started here three months ago, and I have been treated very well. I'm going to have an opportunity to implement all the technology that I have learned. There is also new technology that I have developed by myself. I had a girlfriend in Caracas, but when I told her my plans to leave, she left a month later. Subsequently, I found out that she had married her previous boyfriend from Maracaibo, another city in Venezuela. Those actions confirmed that she was not meant for me. What other proof did I need? On the plane to Bucharest, I met Mihaela, a really special Romanian girl. She is very attractive, but I am afraid of showing my interest in her; rejection is painful. I have no doubt that I'm affected by my breakup and the depressing life I have led. Who knows? Maybe there is a future genuine lover in my life. It's difficult to tell at this early stage and in such a restrictive environment as Iran. We can't take a chance. I told my manager that I had had a problem with an Iranian engineer. He said that the chances of meeting him were one in 80 million, but he was wrong.*

I'd better get dressed, and join the group downstairs at breakfast.

Downstairs in dining room, Mihaela saw some of the delegation members having breakfast. She sat alone and suddenly was approached by a female hotel employee, identified by the hotel pin on her dress. Mihaela was then led to a side room and told to wait. A moment later three men came in to ask for her passport, which she had in her purse. They proceeded to ask questions related to her function in the Romanian delegation. They spoke in understandable English. They wanted to see evidence of the magazine she worked for, and she said that she had some copies in her room. One of the men went out immediately to look for it. Then they asked to see her notebook, and she readily agreed. They saw her notes on the videos from the day before, they took pictures of her notes, and when the man came back with a copy of the *Romanian Petroleum Digest*, she showed him her name and picture in the editor section. They kept the copy of the magazine. Then they asked what her relationship was to Rafael Godoy.

She froze for an instant and told him that she wasn't feeling well last night, and since Rafael was the only single member of the delegation, she had asked him to stay in her room.

They asked, "Did you know him before this meeting?"

"No, we met on the airplane."

"Why do you speak English so well?"

Well, it was evident that if they thought I was speaking English well, their English was not very good. Then they asked me to give them a photocopy of everything I planned to write about the Iranian oil industry. I asked them if they were from the petroleum council.

They answered that the answer was not necessary; they were asking the questions. "This is an Islamic country, and nonmarried people cannot be in same room alone, even if they are not Islamic."

I relaxed a little, as this seemed to be about morals, not spying. I asked them if any of the officials at the petroleum council were US educated. Two of them hurriedly rushed out of room, and they sent in the woman who had brought me there. She sat with me silently, and fifteen minutes later I was dispatched into a car to a very old building near the hotel. Since I understand Farsi, I heard them use language that was surprisingly obscene, but they seemed to be very low-level officers. There I was met by Hamid, the petroleum specialist. He offered a handshake, which was a total surprise. He was gigantic; my guess was that he was almost seven feet tall, and fat. He looked like a scary monster out of a fairy tale. He asked me why I had asked to see him. I told him that I needed to interview someone who spoke English well. That's why I asked for a US-educated oil engineer. He seemed to relax and told me that if I wanted, I could remove my veil. He said he was a modern man and far from the fundamentalist philosophy. That helped explain why we were alone.

"I understand you can't be alone with a woman?"

"Yes, you are right! But don't worry; I'm the boss here. Nobody would dare inform on me.

I took off the veil and released my bundled hair. His response was not subtle.

"You are so pretty!" At this moment, I knew I had a way to save Rafael from possible future harsh treatment. My impact on Hamid further assured me that my beauty was an asset if used properly and carefully. This was going to be a very challenging situation. I accepted an invitation to his apartment, and he explained that his sister would be present. He offered what he called "an excellent American meal." I told him that I had never eaten an American meal but would like to try it. In his conversation he referred to the fact that he might be transferred to London, and he needed a personal secretary. That was followed up by the offer of an excellent salary, "much more than what you are making at the magazine." As a gesture of good faith, he told me that I did not need to continue to watch all the boring videos. I was so surprised that he could be so charming.

He continued by saying, "I can show you everything myself, things you can and can't write about that happen here!"

I told him I was afraid he would get into trouble with the state security. This was my way of probing to find out just how powerful he was.

His response was, "Don't worry. My brother is the head of that department. I do what I want."

He spoke so nicely to me as we went out to breakfast with his secretary as a companion. He whispered to me, "She only speaks Farsi, so it's no problem!"

He thinks he is fully aware of the players and their abilities. There is a lot he does not know. I'm also clear that there is a lot more to know about him and who he really is under his polished presentation. I have an ugly picture of him from Rafael's experiences and his initial attempt to be intimidating to the Romanian group I am traveling with. Let the show continue!

CHAPTER 61

ONCE FREE THERE IS NO TURNING BACK

nfatuation is like a narcotic. Constantin could only sleep for 2 hours that night after meeting Isabella. The next morning they had breakfast together and got to know each other. Too much excitement in such a short time. Isabella was the light of his life! He told her everything about himself, except one important detail, and she shared the facts of her life with him. She talked about the numerous men who attempted to date her and the many embarrassing moments in her life. She spoke about her decision to study in New York at Columbia University. But now she was not sure where her future would take her. "These moments are so special, I'll never forget them, and I want them to continue forever."

He felt the pressure of his responsibility to the family. Because of that, he had to excuse himself and continue his search for a job for Loana. Life and love had taken over, and

Dimitru had proposed to Daniella that night. She immediately accepted. Constantin had to concede to the feelings that were between them. He considered it a fortunate happening; he loved his sister Daniella, and he loved Dimitru like a brother. Now he would formally be a brother-in-law. The couple's next step was planning on how and when to tell their parents.

Constantin had made an appointment at a boutique hotel that was owned by an English billionaire family. He was properly dressed to meet the manager, and he had brought a letter from Mrs. Green introducing him as a close friend of her son. He explained what he needed and shared a photo of his sister Loana with the manager. He spoke of her ability to speak some Mandarin, Romanian, and English but that she had no hotel experience. She was an incredible worker, very punctual, and a fast learner. The manager explained that the hotel needed a person in the maintenance department at this point in time. She could be trained in a few days, but unfortunately the opening was for the night shift only. He assured Constantin that as time passed and she acquired more experience, he would move her to a day job. The pay, he said, was the highest in the market and had health and dental benefits as well as two weeks' vacation a year. Overtime was available if she wanted it. She could start on Monday. The picture and the letter from Mrs. Green were enough proof of her presentability. The hotel clients were VIPs, and he quietly added that at night there was some work only for the very fast clients, where she could make significant money. Then he winked at Constantin to make him understand: "for the clients that come for a quickie." He left full of hope that Loana's part of the plan had just been arranged.

When Loana saw her brother smiling and happy at the front door, she knew that that was the moment to go talk to him. "Constantin, I'm so happy for you. I'm so happy for Daniela. I want you to know I'm not staying here. I just called Mrs. Green to tell her I'm leaving for Hong Kong. She gave the name and telephone of someone she knew there. I also have a phone number that Mrs. Lee gave me that belongs to her husband's good friend who works in a very good hotel."

Constantin stopped her. "Wait one moment, no need to go so far. I've gotten you an excellent job in that boutique hotel Mrs. Green mentioned here in London. You start on Monday. The hotel here is full of wealthy clients, and some come for a sexual interlude. Those are the ones we are interested in."

She became very sad, and she started to cry. She refused to accept the London position, and she threatened to buy herself a ticket and return to Bistriţa. She had developed into an independent woman who could not be subjugated even to Constantin's will.

Even so, Constantin tried to calm her down. He was shocked and had to gather his thoughts. "Wow, what am I going to do now?" He wanted to consult with Dimitru, but he was out with Daniela. Maybe it's a Romanian trait this instant falling in love. He hugged Loana and told her, "Leave for Hong Kong, and do your part of my plan there. I love you, dear sister. I'm sorry I made you cry!" They hugged, and she left on her own to go to the travel agency to meet Mrs. Green. Constantin was impressed by Loana's independence, strength, and dedication to success in life—on her own terms. Dear diary, *where is Joko? I can't get him out of my mind. Did he find Mrs. Lee, and get my message? Will he travel the world for me? Life holds many questions, and now I have no answers.*

CHAPTER 62

JOKO IS FIRING ON ALL CYLINDARS

The detective said he was from Ukraine, a country whose boundaries shifted many times in the last century. He was a little unclear about his description of exactly where he called home. It seemed that he was very sure of himself when it came down to the first step in my ultimate goal of finding Loana, the business of finding a student by the name of Constantin Wood. He told me his fee and contractual conditions. In addition he was very clear that there were no guarantees in his line of work. I agreed to everything, and I insisted that I needed to follow him as the case progressed. He wasn't too enthusiastic about the idea but accepted this condition.

As I was sitting in his office, I received a call from Toyota Corporate. They wanted information about my app and were willing to buy my patent immediately without revision if it lived up to what they were told. Of course, there would be further testing, but if it held up to the claims, I could name my price.

Life is amazing. Here everything was happening at once. I could not speak freely and told them that I would call back in ten minutes. After my call the detective seemed to be in a hurry. There was no issue with payment since my friend's father had guaranteed payment. He said he would phone me later. Upon leaving I told the detective that I would e-mail him all the important information that would allow him to begin the tracking process.

I left his office and called Toyota back. I had a direct phone number, and they answered immediately, at which point I continued with the Toyota executive. I asked him how he had obtained my cell number, which only a handful of people had. He said he didn't know, but they knew my name and e-mail, and they had Toyota dealers in Romania. We spoke briefly, but since this was going to be a life-changing discussion, I needed to be better prepared for it. Catching my breath, I called my father and told him of all the inquiries and the dinner at his friend's house. I told of the incredible welcome I was given by he and his wife. My father then shared with me that one of his secretaries' husbands worked at the Toyota dealership, and she had my number for sure. At that point I understood how vulnerable information is and how many sources were porous when it came to privacy. The US newspapers were full of President Trump's many problems with everything private getting out through so many leaks. In my case it was my dad's secretary. I laughed at the comparison. I decided to call Mrs. Lee, just in case Loana had by any possible chance called her. But no, she hadn't. What I couldn't know was that the next day she would call Mrs. Lee to tell her she was on her way to Hong Kong and to say good-bye. Unfortunately and ironically five minutes after she finished the call and told Loana that I was looking for her, Mrs. Lee's purse was snatched by a fast-moving young boy, and from his clothing, he seemed to be a Gypsy!

Joko decided to go to the passport office, so he took some passport photos at a local shop. The photo-shop owner gave him unasked-for advice. He smiled and said, "When you go, call this number, and Daisy will meet you outside the building. Then you give her an envelope with one hundred euros. This is the envelope, and along with the money, also place your two photos and a copy of your ID card along with it. Wait on the street outside the office, and she will call you in a few minutes to pay the national passport fee and have your fingerprints taken. Following that you will get your passport ten minutes later."

"Why are you telling me this?"

"Well, do you think I can make a living just taking passport photos? She is my daughter, and with one hundred euros per passport, we make a living. You're not a child; you should know by now that anything involving the government bureaucracy involves an 'extra' in Romania."

I understood, and when I got to the passport office, there was a mile-long line. At that point I appreciated his advice, and I decided to call Daisy. I had my passport in twenty-five minutes. That's the way most countries in the third world function. It had never mattered to me before, but my life was changing with lightning speed. I needed all the life lessons I could gather. Even so, I hated to support these illegal bad habits, but I needed a visa for China, and this was the "real" world!

The Chinese consulate was empty. I was the only applicant for a visa to Hong Kong, but when I showed my passport, I was informed that if I stayed less than ninety days, I did not require a special visa. I decided I had no need to apply. I found out that the detective had not been able to find my objective yet, but he was on the case. Therefore, I decided to call my father's friend. He reminded me of my next day's appointment with Mr. Agnelli. I asked myself if I should go or not. Then I thought, why not explore all possibilities in both areas love and business? Maybe I, or the detective could approach Loana's parents.

CHAPTER 63

CUPID STRIKES TWICE

"**H**ello, Father, I have some exciting news for you and Mother. Please push the speaker button so she can hear too. Mama, do you hear me?"

"Yes, yes, my Constantin!"

"You won't believe this. Sit down; it might be too much. I met an American girl, I am deeply in love with her, her name is Isabella, and she is lovely. Mama, are you there?"

"Yes, son, I'm here. Do you know what you are doing?"

"Yes, and life is happening quickly. Daniela is engaged to my friend Dimitru, and they are madly in love."

Father said, "I knew it."

Mother continued. "I liked him the second I saw him. We knew if he had the character qualities to impress you, he must be quite a young man!"

"More good news—you both are ready to move as well. Please sell or give away everything immediately. We want you to fly to Bucharest in three or four days. The store does not have too much merchandise. Forget it; give it away. We don't need money; we don't need anything. Just put on your best clothes, and don't bring anything. Oh yes, bring the passports and any photos of us that you might have as well as our birth certificates and our diplomas."

"Son, Loana and Mihaela, what can you tell me about them?"

"Loana is on her way to Hong Kong, and Mihaela is in Washington, DC, and she will call soon.

"Getting back to yourselves, when you leave, go to this address in Bucharest: 345 Vis Fatole, near the Museum of Modern Art. Take an Uber like I taught you. We will contact you soon. I love you! Good-bye!"

They were sitting and couldn't get up. The excitement was overwhelming, and so was the worry. Yet they had no idea of what more was waiting ahead. Change was in the air and affecting every member of their family. They had waited a lifetime for this activity, and now here it was!

CHAPTER 64

LADY LUCK SMILES

Joko started his morning with a workout in the hotel's gym in Bucharest, the same as he usually did in Bistriţa. He would run ten kilometers every morning and do thirty minutes of heavy lifting. Since arriving in Bucharest, his thoughts had sent him to the imaginary world of the future. He envisioned being with Loana every moment of his life, and that included his gym time. It's incredible how one person attracts you so deeply that everything around you becomes her. He had a certain strange feeling and hope that Loana was thinking of him also. How strange are all these moments. You know you are going to be close, but you don't know how or when it's going to happen.

Arriving he found Mr. Agnelli's office was truly impressive. His company's building was one of the tallest in Bucharest. It was near the Basarab Tower, located in the center of commerce.

As he waited for his appointment, he again felt a chill go

up his spine. Something made him aware of the future. *He wondered, what am I doing here? What am I asking, and how can I best use this interview?* Then his thoughts raced in another direction. *That detective who seemed so sure of himself. Was he on the job, or had he taken a siesta, like they do in Latin America?* He overheard from the secretary's phone conversation that Mr. Agnelli had a very busy day. He had set aside only five minutes to attend to him. At first he felt like leaving, when all of a sudden a big strong man approached him and introduced himself.

"Hi, are you Mr. Joko?"

"Yes, glad to meet you."

"Mr. Gavidescu, my close friend, insisted I meet you and listen to you. Come to my office. Girls, two cups of coffee, please." He put his arm around me as if I was a friend or family. He was dynamic and charismatic, to say the least. I went into a dialogue explaining everything about my invention. All of a sudden, he called his secretary and told her, "Cancel my next two appointments, and no calls please."

This intrigued me. What's on his mind? I told him about the amateur video I had made of my invention. He insisted on seeing it also. He then asked me for permission to share the information with his head chemist and petroleum engineer. He had them called into the office. After a thirty-minute conversation, they were totally impressed and asked if we had applied for a patent. Mr. Agnelli interceded, and said, "Of course!"

After the chemist left, Mr. Agnelli called his lawyer. The

company was so big they had their own legal department. He gave the lawyer instructions for an urgent patent application search. With my permission, a nondisclosure form was hastily produced and signed by the attorney, by Mr. Agnelli, the petroleum engineer, and the chemist. They were the ones that had already proven the viability of this invention. Mr. Agnelli said, "Joko, this is great. You might not know that you have a fortune in your hands. How do you want me to proceed?"

"I don't know yet." I showed him all the e-mails I had received from the companies and the unsolicited one from Exxon. Well, I never thought that my friend Gavidescu was going to send me such a surprise.

"Do you want to offer a small part of your invention? Do you want to sell the invention? Do you want me to help you?"

At that moment, the secretary called him and said, "I'm sorry to disturb you, but it's your son, Dimitru, and it's urgent."

"Sure, put him on." When Joko made a gesture to leave the room, Mr. Agnelli said, "Stay."

Dimitru began. "Papa, I have just asked Daniela to be my wife."

"What? How did that happen! Oh my God! Congratulations!"

"I just wanted you to know. Also amazing is that Constantin fell in love with Isabella, Mother's aunt's niece."

"That's impossible. She only arrived in London two days ago, didn't she?"

"Yes, the impossible has become possible. Where is my mother? She doesn't answer the phone."

"She is out jogging with one of her friends."

"Are you going to have lunch with her?"

"Yes."

"OK call me, but let me be the one to surprise her. Father, I'm so happy."

"So am I, my dear son, so am I."

Joko congratulated him and gave him a high five.

Mr. Agnelli's emotion was visible. He told him, "Joko, I'm sorry I made you go through this very private moment. I did not expect this. We only have one son, and he is the biggest treasure of our life. Now he will marry, and we hope to have grandchildren. This is so incredible. I'm happy to be with such a person as you to share this moment of sublime happiness."

Joko was definitely moved. This man transformed from a highly absorbing and strong personality to a grateful, humble, and happy father. His son had just chosen a bride. An incredible and sincere transformation indeed.

"Joko, where are you from?"

"Bistriţa."

"Oh really? So is my future daughter-in-law. It's a small city, but it has a huge future potential. It seems Bistriţa has produced a genius like you."

"Thank you, Mr. Agnelli. You are being too kind with your words." I guess my sincerity was visible.

"Where are you staying? What are your plans? How will I contact you?"

"I am here in Bucharest, trying to find someone to lead me to the woman I love."

"OK, here is my private cell phone. Please do not share this with anyone. Give me yours, so I can call you as soon as the patent is placed in Romania and internationally. Then we can get together to weigh the options. He called in his secretary and told her to cancel all his appointments, and he let her know that Mr. Joko had total priorities. "Treat him like my son." Suddenly both business and love make for strange bedfellows for both men.

CHAPTER 65

FROM THE HIGHS TO THE LOWS

R afael thought *here I am in Tehran and I never expect to meet a woman like Mihaela. When I left Mihaela's room, I went to my room and readied myself for the day. My experience with her was definitely unique. Never before had I confided in a strange woman to this degree. I had been asked to stay in a woman's room, and I stayed dressed. I was also shocked that I did not even attempt any sexual advances. This was not the Rafael that I had ever been. Something had changed. There had been many women, but prior to this, I had not been so physically close to such a beautiful woman, dressed in black, with a gorgeous face and an incredible figure. In such a brief time I had become both physically close to her and emotionally intimate with her. Being where we are, there are so many restrictions and so many possible problems. I had to move slowly and not follow my natural inclinations.* When I went down to breakfast, I saw Mihaela being taken away by a woman. I asked my coworkers, and they were also disturbed by this occurrence. There was no way for us to inquire about this. When I asked at the front desk, they said they had no knowledge of Mihaela's whereabouts. At that point I became extremely nervous, and I considered the worst possible scenario. She was arrested for sleeping in the same room with a man. They did have cameras everywhere. What could be happening? When the bus arrived and Mihaela did not appear, I pushed the questioning with our guide. At that point he told us that she was interviewing government officials. This calmed me down, but could I trust what they were telling me? The rest of the morning we were occupied by videos and anti-American propaganda. At lunch time, I was separated from my group and was questioned about my job in Romania They had set up a private interview with another US graduate from Texas that same afternoon. That did it; I was in trouble. I know that if necessary, I will have to do something that might create a lot of problems and mess up my job in Romania. I will not permit them to arrest me. I do not want to rot in jail in Iran. I saw my future as very dim. I was trapped here.

CHAPTER 66

NO ONE LEFT BEHIND

I t was difficult with all the changes that had occurred for our children. Now a new life was about to start for us after Constantin›s phone call. We knew that we needed to go to sleep, but I wasn't sure that it was possible. Surprise—we lay down and emotional overload took over and we fell right to sleep.

Bright and early, I was going to go to Fernan's Market and see if he wanted to buy my tobacco supply. Even though Constantin told us to leave everything, I had worked all my life and knew the value of money. Any amount was important, and we only had a few days to turn everything into money. What doesn't help us can help another family. I will go to the church and tell the priest to give away whatever is left in my shop and my house. I will sign the papers and donate the house to the church, and he can use the house for a church family. We had to be grateful, for so many good things were happening for us.

Fernan, a Portuguese immigrant, had opened a market near my store and sold only food. We were not friendly but tolerated each other's presence. I had heard good stories about him from my other customers; therefore, I decided to offer everything I had in stock at cost price. I prepared all the invoices for him to see. My son told us to organize our move quickly. We only had three or four days to close up an entire life's work. For me, that is very difficult. Sophy, my wife, doesn't understand that she must set her sights on the future. I also have some gold hidden in a box under the floorboards in my house. My savings were only in gold. My father taught me that money can become valueless, but gold is forever. You can buy and sell it everywhere in the world. We Gypsies have lived everywhere in the world at one point or another. Our history is that we have been forced to move often on little or no notice. We had to run for our lives, and you can carry your gold with you when you can take nothing else. I never told my children; only Sophy knows. If I go to London, I will put it in a bank. I must also give this to my children. If they marry, we must give them gold.

The travel agency where my girls bought the airline ticket was near the bus stop, and we went very early. We bought two tickets for the next day. I wanted to see how the Uber system worked in my phone. It only worked near the bus stop. They say that other places have no Wi-Fi. I don't understand all these new things, Wi-Fi, PayPal, whatever. I tested pushing the button, and then I must have done something wrong. So I went into a shop, and the owner was nice and explained it all again. It's a good thing that I tested it; now I am ready. Tomorrow he told me if we come to his store he will call an Uber for me from my phone. My airplane was to leave at one o'clock, and we both were afraid of flying. It was to be our first time. Our children were already experts. Sophy reminded me that we probably had to repay Dimitru's family all the money they lent us. I did not know how much we would need to repay, but we could never repay the friendship, help, and support we were receiving. I did have gold, and I would be glad to give that, but we would always be in their debt.

MONEY AND POWER DO NOT BUY EVERYTHING

H amid was very attracted to this Romanian woman, who was exquisite. He only dreamed of having a woman like her. He thought through how he was going to make her his wife. There were going to be many problems to resolve because there were vast cultural differences. She was also very educated since she was part of this delegation and writes for a journal. Being an engineer, and Western trained, he began to parse the questions that he would have to confront.

First I need to make her want me, and then I have to convince her to convert. My family would never accept my taking a non-Muslim. Third is her place in my society, or whether we need to move to a western country. She seems worth the sacrifice; I have to win her over. I'm going to show her how important I am. All women fall in love with a man who has power. My brother, the minister of defense, will help me. However, I really don't need his help; everyone knows me. Here in Iran, the last name Hamid opens all the doors. I told my secretary to cancel all my appointments and have my assistant,, interview the other Romanians. We don't trust very easily, and this is an exploratory delegation.

I decided to drive her around the city and show her how doors open for me. The guides were notified that there was no need worry about this member of the delegation, that she was with me. I explained that I would be interviewed by her and that I would take care of her. Furthermore, I had given an order to permit her to visit high-security sites accompanied by me. Because of the classified nature of these locations, I would do the driving. A driver was not permitted to go where we were visiting.

She suspected that it was his way of flirting and attempting to impress her. Mihaela decided to play along, that way she was safe, and so was Rafael. Owing to her well-trained memory, she silently identified the location of many high-security facilities. During his explanations, she secretly pressed the recording app several times to send out the information. At one site there were military airplanes, and there she asked him to take a selfie with her. He was so blinded with infatuation that he loved that idea. He only hesitated for a minute but let it happen. As she used her phone camera, she inclined the camera to photograph many other important elements of the installation. He started taking selfies with his camera, of her with him. It was evident that he was smitten with her looks and charm.

Everywhere he went he created a commotion and demanded respect from all the military officers. He did not realize it, but there was resentment for his manner and tone. None could believe how he held and fraternized with a woman who wasn't his wife, and here in public. Owing to this insult and disrespect of the both secular and religious rules, one commander decided to report him to his superior. The superior, a friend of the minister, called Hamid to let him know that he was just reported and by whom. Hamid went back immediately after he was informed, and he had the base commander arrested for treason.

Mihaela, who understood what was happening because of her Farsi comprehension, did not like what she saw but continued to smile, even though she realized what a brutal and cruel man lay below the suave and polished exterior that he presented. During all these journeys to petroleum deposits, refineries, and armed installations, she was able to memorize the relative location or take selfies. She sent all this valuable information with the click of the button.

Hamid had plans for the next day. They would take a plane to a secret base near an unidentified oil refinery. He was feeling his power and influence, of which he had convinced himself. His plan was to move slowly but surely toward what he wanted with her. In his initial step, he took her to her hotel and tried to hug her. He did not want to spook her or frighten her, so it remained a hug.

Mihaela was not blinded by this display. For her it was difficult to accept since she knew so much more about him than he showed that day. This was her mission and her attempt to shield Rafael; therefore, she had no choice. How little would he accept, and how slowly would he go, until she could not tolerate it? How would this end safely for all? Hamid was used to having his way with no opposition. It was clear from what he did to Rafael that underneath he was ruthless.

Before Hamid let her go, he said, "Dear Mihaela, I gave you my cell phone, but don't call me directly. Use WhatsApp. Do you have WhatsApp?"

"No I don't." I can download it now.

"WhatsApp is impossible to record, so I think it's safe to talk if you need me. Another thing, the only places the hotel doesn't have wires, microphones, and cameras are the bathrooms. The halls are not safe either. This is the hotel we use only for foreign delegations. Right now your delegation is the only one present. I will call you in the morning. Don't tell anyone where I took you, please. It's not permitted, and no one should know! Is that understood?" he said, with a lot of emphasis on warning her.

"Understood!"

CHAPTER 68

DIMITRU TALKS BUSINESS AND FUTURE

N ow that Loana had left London for Hong Kong, everyo-
nes feelings were out in the open. Daniela did not let
Dimitru out of her sight. They took great pleasure in
just being together, as young lovers do. They went everywhere
together and got together with Isabella and Constantin day
and night. They were all inseparable, according to Isabella's
aunt, who, after seeing the reality of the situation, decided
to take an airplane back to her home in Manhattan. She
had a sense of fulfillment with Isabella planning a life with
Constantin, a fine young man.

That evening, the four of them were going to plan their
futures together, not only their futures together but their economic futures. Constantin could not permit his friend, and
future brother-in-law, to maintain him. Dimitru wasn't the
type to depend on his parents for money without offering

them something in return. Mixed in with the love was a deep sense of reality. That is what demanded they address the issue that Constantin's plan was meant to resolve: how to live an advantaged life. Right now they had only an ethic of hard work. They had discussed a series of ideas intended to make their company prosper.

Dimitru had already talked to his mother and explained everything to her. She, as well as his father, were as happy that their only son had chosen a mate for life. Daniella spoke to them, and they saw the joyful couple together on Facetime through their iPhone. They simply loved his choice. They would soon share the intended plans, and the family would get together in either London or Bucharest.

Dimitru told his love, "My mother wanted to give me her engagement ring to give to you, Daniela, but I told her that I will give you a ring when I earn the money to buy one."

On the other side of the couple, Daniela had also spoken to her parents, just before they got on the airplane to Bucharest. She told Dimitru, "Let me tell you how happy they were. I have never heard Mom and Dad so relaxed, joyful, and uplifted as they were for us. When they asked me about my two sisters, I didn't have any news yet, but at least I had our good news for them."

That evening, the four of them went to a wine shop and bought some Romanian cabernet sauvignon, Castel Huniade 2011, and some excellent Greek feta cheese and crackers. Then the four went to a small park on the Thames River on a hidden gully. They had plastic glasses, and I brought a tablecloth from the apartment. They sat down, put some romantic music on an iPhone, and enjoyed the view. The four of them felt a unique closeness.

Isabella had also announced to her astonished parents her very fast and effective romance with "the most magnificent man I ever met." She also introduced Constantin to them on Facetime, and he spoke to them and said, "You have sent me the angel of my dreams, Isabella."

They started crying with joy. They were comforted since they heard from Isabella's aunt that he was a fine young man, endorsed by Dimitru and his family. It was a great beginning. Isabella told them that she did not think she would return to Columbia University at this time, but she said that as soon as everything was clear, they would fly to New York so they could meet Constantin. They asked why they couldn't come to meet him where they were. She said, "OK, I'll let you know as soon as possible."

Constantin and Dimitru, both were very capable in mathematics, and that opened all kinds of business fields to them.

Dimitru said, "I want you to be an equal partner, If I need a loan, my father will give it to me. We both will repay him. Now we also have our future wives as partners. Both are smart and capable. This is going to be a business with four partners."

"Yes, let's drink to that."

And drink they did in a responsible way!

CHAPTER 69

PATIENCE IS A VIRTUE AS JOKO LEARNED

After his amazing session with Mr. Agnelli, Joko decided to call the detective again. He was asked to have patience. He said he had a lead but was not going to give Joko information until it was confirmed. He needed to relax, think, and wait to be called. Having done this many times before, the detective knew that a forlorn lover can be impulsive and rush to follow a trail that may not lead anywhere.

Joko headed to the banks of the Oticuli River, to a tranquil and relaxing area. Time goes by very slowly when one is in a rush. I certainly was in a rush to find the woman I wanted to make a life with. If what Mrs. Lee told me was true, her family's objective was to marry her off to a wealthy person. This was a very disturbing thought. I knew that I had to find her before she made a serious error with her life, and mine. The twilight of nightfall and the lights across the river gave a glimmer of hope. He wanted so badly to know what to do next. That's when his phone rang. In the excitement of the moment, he tripped and almost fell into a gully right by the river.

The detective, said, "I just received confirmation that Constantin Wood finished his course at the Technical Institute, and I found out that he was an excellent student. That's not all. I interviewed the admissions secretary, and she let me take a picture from his student folder. I then went back to the campus, and when I showed his photo to some girls at the cafeteria, they immediately identified him and said he hangs out with Dimitru something, a real rich friend. She didn't know anything else. I pursued the matter, and I went to the registrar and asked for the address. He gave his home address as being in Bucharest. With some prodding they gave me the address in care of Mr. Dimitru Agnelli, another student here."

When Joko heard that, he excitedly thanked the detective and said case was resolved. He called Mr. Agnelli, yet he decided not to tell him of his newly acquired interest in his son, Dimitru.

"Hi, Mr. Agnelli, I hope I'm not disturbing you."

"No, not at all" was his response.

"I overheard you on the phone talking to your son. Is his name Dimitru?"

"Yes, it is."

"Well, do you think he might be interested in participating with me in my project? If he is going to marry shortly, he might need to develop his own business interest. Since you were so enthusiastic with my invention, I thought of him. I need someone young and energetic and with his connections as a working advisor. In fact, I plan to be in London tomorrow. Is he there?"

"Yes, he is there! And what a fabulous idea! Mr. Joko, you are an angel that God sent to us! Thank you. I'll connect with him right now on his cell phone, and you can make your offer to him in person. I'll let him know to expect your call."

Joko went straight to his hotel, picked up his small carry-on, checked out, and went to the airport. He thought, I'm going to get the first flight out to London, even if it's via Singapore. Loana, I'm closer to you! What a relief—there is a connection to finding Loana, and it is through a channel that is important to her: her brother and his friend Dimitru. I am free to search the world for who and what I want.

CHAPTER 70

MANAGED ENCHANTMENT

Mihaela thought, I'm in a tough spot I am trapped here. This man is interested in me, and he definitely was serious about establishing a relationship. I'm just not sure how far he will go to force a connection with me. He is a powerful man, from a culture that does not regard the feelings of women. It is a male-dominated society, and I have to keep up a facade for nine more days. How I got into this, I don't know. I am a victim of my looks. My mother used to tell all of us to show as little of our sexuality as possible. "All men are the same; they all want the same thing. Be careful. Don't lead them on." She had always said that our father was an exception. He was a man of one woman—her. We all believed in her philosophy.

Now I'm in Iran, a society where woman cover up totally, and I'm covered up everywhere. I have still attracted this monster. Doesn't he see himself? Or maybe he didn't see the American movie *Beauty and the Beast,* but I sense that there is more to this beast than his appearance? This was wonderful for my work as an agent, and the material I had sent back was valuable. I need to focus on walking a tightrope, leading him on without committing to him. I need to leave this awful society as soon as I can. I officially know there are cameras and microphones everywhere except the bathrooms. Maybe he said that to trick me. He must have been told of my encounter with Rafael. No, I don't think he would deceive me; he is authentic with me. He tries his utmost to be nice and kind. Sometimes he can't control his authoritarian tendency, like when he warned me not to tell anyone where he had taken me.

It is late, after nine o'clock, and I need to speak to someone. If it's safe to use the WhatsApp, should I call Constantin? I had better not. I'll send a positive report to my boss to support my cover story of being a reporter. I'll write to Rafael's WhatsApp. No, I will call Hamid first, since I need to further his interest in me and my access to classified information. I went into the bathroom, put on the shower, and called him.

He immediately answered. I said, "Hamid, I want to thank you for the wonderful day you gave me." He was impressed with my thankful appreciation. I wished him a good night, and he told me to have breakfast with the Romanians, but he followed that with, "Don't take the bus with the group. I will pick you up at ten o'clock."

I immediately texted Rafael and told him to go into bathroom, where I knew I could safely call him. Rafael was overjoyed to hear from me, but he was alarmed by what I told him later in the conversation. He said that the complete delegation was very concerned that something had happened to me. I explained everything fast and to the point, speaking in general terms, and I didn't tell him where he had taken me. I warned him about the confirmed cameras and microphones everywhere. I tried to let him know that I was doing this to keep him safe. He deeply appreciated the comments, and then we were silent for a few seconds, each one hearing our breath and our sighs.

The next morning, Hamid arrived promptly. He drove straight to a government airport. He bragged that he was also a pilot but wanted to be with me, and therefore he would not pilot the plane himself. He told me he wanted to share the beautiful sights of the Iranian countryside in a very clear attempt to convince me of the beauty of his country. He ventured to sit as close as possible and touched my arm continuously. I decided that it was part of my obligation to accept his touchy manners for the moment. I worried that it might lead to something more. After all, being in public did not inhibit him. I had seen what he had done to the base commander who reported him. He had no fear and no need to be afraid. He took me to a secret nuclear station and let me interview two scientists. He translated, even though they had been prepared for this visit, and they sang the party song. They explained that they were engaged in the peaceful use of nuclear energy for the benefit of humankind.

I took notes and secretly recorded most of the conversations and sent them out immediately. I took some pictures when he went to the bathroom and sent them out. When we went for lunch to a missile-launching base, he told me that he was a very rich man and had a secret account in the Isle of Man (that belonged to Great Britain) and one in Andorra, a small country between Spain and France. He did not say how he got so rich. He hinted that whoever becomes his wife will enjoy his riches, and his future children would go to England to study. He said he was Islamic but did not believe in all the extreme religious elements.

We returned to my hotel after a very tiresome day. He wanted my opinion on Islam and wanted to know if I would marry a Muslim. I answered that I didn't know very much about Islam and said that my parents taught me to respect all religions. When I fall in love, religion will not be an issue for me. Furthermore, I said I don't think religion is important. He seemed to like that answer and told me as much. Hamid said, "I hope that you learn to appreciate how dedicated I am to you. Remember, I'm a very important and influential person here, and that is important for the future. Please call me again tonight." *This seems like a lot more than a friendship.*

CHAPTER 71

A NEW COUNTRY, A NEW LIFE, A NEW FRIEND

For Loana it was a very long flight, but Virgin Atlantic was a great airline, and she arrived fully rested. She immediately took a taxi to Mrs. Lee's husband's relatives, who were expecting her. They had been alerted by Mrs. Lee's husband that she would arrive sometime in the near future. Tomasso and his wife were so very nice. They offered their extra room and insisted she eat and go to sleep so that she could deal with the jet-lag issue. The next morning Tomasso took Loana with him to talk to his boss at the prestigious Hong Kong Ritz Carlton. He worked there as a butler and was very happy with his job. He had a wonderful reputation at the hotel, and with his recommendation his manager gave her a job as a maid. He assigned her to assist a more experienced maid and to use her methods as a model of what was needed to be done. The ability to speak some Mandarin was a plus, along with her facility for English. She was assigned a small room in the employees" quarters, and settled in for the start of work the next day. As fate would have it the private tailor from the hotel needed an assistant for the day. Loana was available and gladly accepted the assignment. There was a very important client of the hotel chain, Mr. Chong, who needed some new clothing ASAP.

Two weeks later Tomasso called Loana at work to share that he was being asked questions by private detectives. Loana understood that it probably had to do with Mr. Chong's insistence on having her around him. He was such a nice and well-intentioned man. The hotel tailor told me that he was a prominent citizen and everyone respected him. He sent me personal gifts during those two weeks and that was concerning. I decided to gather some information about him, his family, and his children. I was told that his wife had passed away, and he was now a desperately lonely man. When I inquired about his family, he became very happy, thinking I wanted a relationship with him. I had to be straightforward with him and tell him, "I'm a young person. I'm here to make a living." He became so animated and excited. He said that his daughter, Pricilla, was the only family he had, and he would arrange for me to get together with her.

He was very happy. He believed that his daughter would convince Loana to be with him even if it meant just to be his platonic partner. He didn't know why he had fallen for a young, darling girl. He considered the discrepancy in their ages and how that would be perceived. Pricilla received a very incomplete and unclear report from her detective, Pierce Lee, about this young woman, Loana. Next, Pricilla's father called her and informed her that a new friend of his, who happened to be a very young woman, wanted to meet her. In addition, her father said that this young woman wanted to talk with her.

Pricilla became very nervous; she imagined the worst! She, like her deceased mother, were always afraid of young foreign men and women because they'd had a number of unhappy experiences to support that concern. Pricilla's ex-husband, also a foreigner, enticed her and manipulated her. He too was too young for her, and all he wanted was money. She was lucky to discover his negative intentions before he stole from her father's investments. Pricilla thought, I need to be prepared for a ransom ultimatum from her. I will give her a chance to talk. Tell her I'll meet her at the hotel. I am really afraid of her seeing the degree of my father's infatuation with her because the price will go up!

Loana received a message that afternoon: At 6:00 p.m. Mrs. Pricilla Chong invites you to join her for coffee in the restaurant's private room.

Loana had no idea what to say, but she had to put a stop to these presents and to his intentions. At exactly six o'clock, Mrs. Chong walked in, dressed in fine clothes and smelling of a perfume that was so mild and yet a scent so enhancing that it spread all over the room. She was really pretty, and she seemed to be angry and ready to fight.

Loana seized the opportunity to speak first. "I'm in love

with a young Romanian man, and I hope he comes to Hong Kong. I would love for you and your father to meet him." This initial statement immediately calmed Pricilla down, and her facial expression changed totally. She became friendly and gave Loana a kiss and hug. Loana relaxed. She was right. Now she hoped that Mr. Chong would understand.

"Have you told my father?"

"No, I have really spoken very little with him, and we have only talked about Romania. But he sends me presents three times a day, and I would like to return them. I suspect or feel he misses your mother, and maybe saw in me a substitute. His loneliness was very evident when I went to meet him with the tailor. Can you explain my situation to him?"

Pricilla, with a big smile, hugged her again and offered her a job in her office and promised to give her future Romanian husband a job in one the many companies her father still managed. "I will help you. Your presence has given my father a new reason to live, and I am sure that he will understand and be happy for you." Pricilla grinned. "How easy it is to uncomplicate an uncomplicated situation."

A series of things happened in the next few days that would change the plan, and Loana's life, forever.

Joko realized that he had become a man of action. He was able to get out on a flight to Paris, followed by a connection to Heathrow, but it was very late. He checked into an airport Radisson, at which point he was extremely tired and took a power nap. At nine o'clock that night, Joko called Dimitru.

When Dimitru answered, he already had been informed by his father that a Mr. Joko was going to contact him with an incredible business idea. The information wasn't specific, but he was told that Joko was the son of one of his best friends. That was enough for his dad, and it was OK with him. Dimitru knew his father never trusted anyone in business. There were too many slick characters.

Joko did not want to ruin his surprise advantage, so he didn't mention Constantin or his Loana, his real target. The arrangement was to meet later in the day at a small wine shop near the temporary London home. Dimitru gave him the address, and then Joko checked into a nearby hotel. Again, he noticed how slow the minutes moved when he wanted them to move like a windmill in a storm. The time arrived, and after a few moments, he identified Dimitru by the photo the detective had sent to his phone. He was tall like his father and just as handsome.

After the introduction preliminaries, it was explained that his partner, Constantin Wood, would arrive in a few moments. They were delayed in traffic along the way. Joko gave a preliminary view of his invention but would be more specific after the partner, Constantin, arrived. With Constantin were Daniela and another young woman, who was introduced as Isabella.

Daniela immediately recognized Joko and hugged him and started crying. "Loana left a few days ago for Hong Kong," she blurted out through tears.

Constantin then recognized him. He looked and presented

himself very differently then when he wore his mechanic overalls. Was this Joko? "Yes, it's me Constantin, my app and all it can do is real." Daniela immediately shared openly that Loana was in love with Joko.

Daniela defended Joko and said, "Well, Constantin, you and Isabella fell in love thirty seconds after meeting. Joko has been around Loana for more than three years. Dimitru fell in love with me thirty seconds after he saw me at the hotel in Bistrita. It took a long time until he dared express his love because of you."

Constantin hugged Joko and said he was sorry for his words. Instead of talking first about the invention, all they spoke about was how to intercept Loana in Hong Kong. Speed was of the essence, but three of the five people did not understand why, and they were not going to be told the rest of Constantin's plan. Loana had not communicated recently, and they had no idea where she was. Daniela got on the Virgin Atlantic Airline website and told Joko that at nine thirty there was a direct flight to Hong Kong with plenty of seats available. They all spent the remaining time together planning and contacting their families, and filling each other in on missing pieces to the puzzle. Then they listened intently to the description of Joko's invention and what it was capable of. They speculated about the implications for all of them in the future. It seemed limitless.

When they spoke to Mr. Agnelli he could not believe the incredible coincidence that had been occurring.

The flight left on time with Joko aboard. He always

thought that he would go around the globe to find his love, and now he actually was doing it. He had to explain to himself as well how he could have loved her from afar and allowed her to leave, never approaching her. He was going to fix that mistake half the world away.

They had not heard from Mihaela, and they were getting worried. In her last contact she had told her parents that she would call in two weeks. A week had already passed.

CHAPTER 72

WASHINGTON PULLS THE STRINGS

R afael received Mihaela's WhatsApp text and then took a risk. For the first time since his arrival in this city, he communicated with his handler to inform them of what was happening with Mihaela and the rest of the delegation. Rafael of course did not know that Mihaela had been sending them recordings and videos of great value. Rafael had been recruited by the US government after he finished his studies in Texas. Initially, they convinced him to work for the US with the agreement that his complete family would receive a special visa to the United States, so they could legally immigrate. His assignment was to keep them informed on what was really happening with all the petroleum industries' funds in Venezuela. Where was the money going? How could this superpower in the oil industry have no money to feed the nation? Why didn't they have money to purchase medicine?

He was to help them discover the biggest misuse of funds in the world. But things got very hot and dangerous for him in Caracas, so he had to be reassigned.

He was sent to Bucharest, waiting for a place where he might be needed. They grasped the opportunity to send him out to the Tehran visit, He was also tasked with the reporting of the events and people who were a part of this delegation. In his report he mentioned Mihaela and her inside track with Hamid. He told them of his fear of being discovered by Hamid, his known enemy. The agency did not think it was an impediment.

What a complicated spot to be in. Mihaela called him to tell him that she was well but extremely nervous whenever Hamid broached his feelings for her. She didn't know what the outcome would be. He told her to be very careful. Of course he couldn't divulge that he was reporting these details that she was sharing with him. A few minutes later, before leaving the safety of the bathroom, he received an order to keep low, avoid going to the next three days' delegation travel. In addition, Mihaela received new activity instructions, and her goal would be to get Hamid to fly to London with her. Rafael couldn't ask why. In this field you never ask why something is being done or ordered. he started worrying about these new orders. Why should he stay behind? And why bring Hamid to London? She was going to have to use some sexual promise in order to lure him out of Iran. He had a very special feeling for Mihaela, and it hurt him that they are using her in this capacity. They told him she was expendable.

All of a sudden, Mihaela received another message: Bathroom. In the bathroom the voice message was short: "Continue selfies with Hamid, entice him to meet you in London. Use whatever excuse a beautiful, intelligent woman can use. —Radu." Then, "Erase this message immediately." She sat down in amazement. *What have I gotten myself into? Should I confide in Rafael? No, that is not possible. I'm alone in this.* She got a hold of herself and proceeded to call Hamid from the bathroom. It was now eight o'clock. She knew what they wanted, but at what price to her? She had to go slowly and carefully. This was all new territory for her.

CHAPTER 73

HOPE ON THE HORIZON

Hamid thought to himself, *even the rich and famous have feelings. I am 34 years old and unmarried*

Life isn't easy growing up in a very religious Islamic Shiite family. They had to be religious because the government did not recognize the existence of a secular life. In fact, the Sunni minority in Iran did not have the same rights. They were discriminated against by the government since Shiites formed vast majority of the population. I had been courting a Sunni girl, but when my father and brother found out, that was the end. My brother had been very successful in the army and was the minister of defense. This was one of the highest and most influential posts in the government. That's why he was so important in the Iranian petroleum industry, and I was his brother. Everyone had to respect me, and everyone was afraid to upset me and risk jail time or worse—hard labor at the worst of prisons.

I am a large man, not a pleasing presence. As a kid I was bullied, but now I am the one in control. I was a very smart student; everyone, including my family, thought I had cheated my way through the university and then through my postgraduate work in Texas. In the United States, my accomplishments proved to everyone that it wasn't cheating. I almost made summa cum laude, which is no easy task. I also reorganized the whole petroleum system in Iran. It was now very profitable, thanks to me. I have been able to save a lot of money, most of it to benefit my family. They caused some big international contracts to get approved, and these contractors gave us a "commission" for our unfaltering help. We had to have the fortune deposited in safe places outside of Iran, of course.

I love the West, the freedom, the liberty, the acceptance of whatever religion you want to belong to. If I ever move to the US or Great Britain, I will probably continue to be a Muslim but not a religious one. In fact, that is my goal. I want to get out of this restricted life. I don't "feel" what I preach or what is preached to me. I believe that everyone has the same rights; it doesn't matter what you believe in. Now this incredible Romanian possibly comes into my life. She is so incredible! I have been trying to impress her, and I will continue to do so. Maybe I have a chance? These Romanians love money and powerful men, and I am both. I have to be careful and erase all those selfies I took with her. I also need to do that on her phone before she leaves for Bucharest. Last night when she called me, she was downright sweet. She actually said she was looking forward to tomorrow to be with me. I need to be with a woman, but since my religion doesn't permit it, I often travel to countries where sex is easily obtained. But with this woman, it's not only carnal lust. I want to take her for life and marry her. I will need to leave Iran, and I'm ready to make the move. I have six days more to implement my seduction of her.

The next day Mihaela went down for breakfast, and Rafael informed the group and the guide that he was feeling very ill and would not join them. The guide reported this to his superiors. After a short wait, he was informed that they would send an officer to accompany him, and if he required medical assistance, it was available. This information was passed on to Hamid's aide. Hamid was informed of this, then he realized that they were talking about his Texas University rival. He knew what he would need to do.

Hamid arrived at the hotel to pick up Mihaela. Instead of waiting for her to come to his car, he got out and waited for her in the lobby. Once the bus left, he asked to go to the back garden. In a far corner, they sat down, and he told Mihaela the story of his two years in Texas and of one of her colleagues from Romania.

"Did you know he is not Romanian? He is Venezuelan. A very bright fellow. I didn't like him, but I admired him because he was as smart as I am, or even smarter. I wanted to kill him when he beat me for the honor at graduation. After giving it some thought, I was going to apologize for all my mean ways. Before I knew it, right after the diploma reception, he disappeared. I later searched for him, and I found out that he had developed an innovative method of drilling for oil that was really impressive. I convinced the Iranian ministry to hire him, but he was already back in his country, working for that corrupt government oil industry. Now, I find out that he is here and is sick. Do you know him?"

"Yes, I know everyone in the delegation."

"I'm going to ask him to come down to speak to me. Here in the garden, there are no microphones, so I'll see if he is receptive to me. He probably fears me, like everyone, except you of course."

She gave him her hand to hold. That act, where she held his hand voluntarily, melted any possible anger, and it changed him. Now his demeanor was nice, humble, and friendly.

When Rafael was summoned, he didn't know what to expect or who he was going to see. When he saw Hamid, his heart started to accelerate; it's beating tripled. He thought, This is it. I am done for! In front of him, his enemy. Oh, why did I come? Damn it, I'm going to die here.

Hamid, with an extended hand, greeted him, Mihaela right by his side. "Dear colleague, nice seeing you."

Rafael was flabbergasted. It seemed that this was a whole different ball game. They spoke for hours and didn't move. Hamid continuously reminded them that this was the safest place to talk. He told him that a job offer with double the salary he was making now was a possibility. Rafael showed interest. It was the thing to do. Mihaela held Hamid's hand, and little by little gained more confidence in the actual situation and the new advantages and possibility of completing her latest order: "Make him meet you in London."

In Washington this situation was being analyzed and the thoughts were exchanged. Radu brainstormed with lieutenant Fellows: "Great expectations were in order. This young girl, Mihaela, is turning out to be a great agent. She recorded and sent everything related through Hamid. This is an incredible chance for us to get someone with such status into our ranks. Rafael has been extremely cautious because of his past with Hamid, and now that is turning into a huge asset. He was just offered a job in the Iranian oil industry. If Mihaela can get him to London or to a Western city, we can definitely approach him with a package that is impossible to refuse."

"I'm not so sure he will accept; he will be afraid to jeopardize his brother's high position. I also believe Mihaela can't be ordered to be his life partner. She is young and has plans for the future."

"I know what you mean, Radu, but this is such an important breakthrough that we might have to blackmail him with the photos he permitted Mihaela to take. Those pictures in the wrong hands would be his downfall, and his family's."

"He won't cooperate," Radu responded. "We had better rush our agreement with Rafael."

"Immigration hasn't answered our petition yet. We need to rush that. Rafael won't accept a position in Tehran without visible action on our part. Will Mihaela continue with us after all the hardships we are causing her? I have a suspicion that there might be an affair brewing between her and Rafael."

"That would complicate our situation," said Radu.

"Yes, Radu, it was a good idea to make Rafael feign being sick; what you predicted happened."

"Yes, but it was very risky. What if Hamid had decided to get rid of him?"

"Those are the chances our professionals must take."

CHAPTER 74

GOOD THINGS
HAPPEN IN PAIRS

ood luck was not confined to Tehran, when Joko arrived at the hotel in Hong Kong, he decided to check in early. Suddenly, he had become a world traveler and had chased his love across the globe. Before this he lived the life of a mechanic. Living in a small, sleepy city, he silently longed for time with Loana. Now he was in another foreign city, seeking the same thing, but he wanted more. He wanted her to be his wife. Joko also wanted to benefit from his unique invention and the new acquaintances he had made along the way. He was so nervous that he wasn't sure what to do first. To refresh, he took a fast shower, changed his clothes, and called to see if a Mr. Tomasso was available, but he wasn't. Next he called the cell number he was given. It was answered by a Chinese voice-mail recording. He decided to go to the Tomassos' home address. On the way down the elevator, it stopped at the mezzanine floor, and the most incredible and blissful moment in his life happened!

Loana walked right into the elevator. Looking at each other in disbelief, they hugged each other, and the rest was history. Words were not necessary. They remained there in a prolonged hug that they wished would never end. After recuperating from the blissful, incredible shock, they decided to WhatsApp their families. Loana's father had no idea that they had such a strong interest in one another. He took the position that if she was happy, so was he. Loana imagined that since they didn't know what was happening with Joko's invention, her parents probably figured, "This is the end of Constantin's plan to get us out pf poverty, but at least Loana seemed so happy." Her parents comforted themselves with the old Gypsy saying, "In life happiness is the most important thing."

Constantin and Daniela were very relieved. It seemed that everything had gone tremendously well, even though the variations on the "plan" caused there to be no plan. They knew the incredible potential of Joko and his invention. This relieved the sisters from the most distasteful aspect of Constantin's plan. Now they would not have to create an unwanted pregnancy with a total stranger for the purpose of blackmail. Reflecting back, Constantin thought sadly that his Gypsy background held him back from other possibilities in life. He couldn't see any other way out for his family or himself. Now life had changed dramatically, and so many opportunities appeared before him.

Seizing the opportunities, they made plans for gathering all the extended family members in London. As far as Constantin could evaluate, his efforts to raise his entire family from a life of poverty and hopelessness were successful. All the family members also agreed that they would fly to London as soon as possible. Loana's boss, the hotel's tailor, wasn't too happy. He would lose his newest and most prized employee. Life was filled with change, and everyone must adjust, they had no choice.

They also called Mrs. Lee to inform her that her help was invaluable and to thank her for all she had done and the role she had played. The next call that Loana made was to Miss Pricilla Chong, her new friend and ally. She wanted to share with her that her dream had come true; Joko had come to Hong Kong. Ms. Chong asked to meet Joko and told her that the situation with her father had been resolved. They had engaged in a very productive conversation about the loss of her mother, his wife, and they began the grieving process together. She reported that her father's mood had picked up and that he could turn to her now when he was depressed, and she could do the same with him. Ms. Chong explained that Loana had done the family a great service and that she had been an honorable young woman. She'd not taken advantage of a man in his lowest moments. Ms. Chong offered to help with whatever Loana and her husband to be ever needed.

CHAPTER 75

THE PRIZE GETS BIGGER

Along with riches, power is part of the treasure at the end of the rainbow.

Rafael had recorded the conversation with Hamid and Mihaela when they were in the garden and sent it all back to Radu. Mihaela had done the same, unaware that Rafael was also employed by the US government.

Suddenly, a security guard came to Hamid and told him, in Farsi, that his office was urgently trying to reach him. He had shut off his phone because he wanted total privacy in the garden. He didn't want interruptions. He called his office and again in Farsi was told something that changed the color in his face to pale; something important was being said to him. He hung up and dispatched the guard. Then he said, "It appears that my brother, the minister of defense, was asked to be a candidate for president."

"That is absolutely incredible."

"I must go. He wants me in his office now! Please do

not—I repeat, do not—share this with anyone." He left hurriedly, and they remained in the garden, looking at each other in amazement. They were participating in this historic moment, and now they realized how close they were to one of highest and most influential men in the country. Rafael excused himself, telling her that he needed the bathroom. She understood, and they both went to their respective rooms. Once there, in the safety of their bathrooms, they both reported back to Radu. Their reports, messages, and conclusions were almost identical: "We might have hit the jackpot."

Radu's instructions to Mihaela followed, with a copy to Rafael: "You are to continue your charade with Hamid. Follow all his prompts, and do as he says. You will be amply rewarded. We agree that this is a major breakthrough for us."

To Rafael, in a privateWhatsApp message, Radu told to him to investigate further the job offer and ask him for time to think about it and make sure that the conditions for traveling freely are part of the deal. In addition, he should make sure to ask for a lot of money to make the decision to accept more logical.

After a few moments, Rafael securely contacted Mihaela: It's six o'clock. Come down, and let's eat together. We haven't even had lunch.

She smiled. She knew how important this was going to be for the United States and the world. On that day Mihaela found her calling. She was going to continue to be an agent for the United States. In addition, she found her adult feminine side. How would she combine these two elements? What would she tell or not tell Rafael? Mihaela was constantly concerned about her family in London. She wondered how the plan was proceeding there, and what her sisters would have to do to project their lives forward.

CHAPTER 76

DEBTS THAT CANNOT BE REPAID

I n London there was deep consideration and discussion: "Constantin, this is our situation: We have achieved incredible things after only one month in London. You and I have found our dream women, and your sister Loana has resolved our business future. Through Loana we have found an amazing opportunity with Joko and his invention. We should be able to develop its potential to the utmost advantage, and this will benefit all the people in the world. We will be responsible for making fuel consumption much cheaper. I hope Joko won't change his mind about the offer to make us his partners. He has been receiving offers without a definite price tag or conditions from everywhere. Offers have come in from the automotive industry and from all the major oil companies. I think that he should retain the controlling interest in the company we need to form. He wants it to be an equal partner situation; that's what he reiterated to me an hour ago. Maybe he should consult with a lawyer first? Joko said that he wants Loana's family to have an equal economic stake in his invention. He is also madly in love with your sister. What a story to tell our grandchildren."

"OK, Dimitru, we all have you to thank. You are the one that gave us the opportunity that we now have."

Daniela added, "That is true! Now our parents are in Bucharest in that really nice apartment that you found for them."

"Yes," said Constantin, "we owe you everything. I promise to repay every last cent. Give me a few months' time after we start to work."

"Dear Constantin, the way I see it, I owe you. I don't know how I'm going to pay you. Through you I found the most incredible woman, a woman only present in my dreams. In addition, through you we have found a business that is going to make us what you have only dreamed of—billionaires, all of us!

"Dimitru, listen, I'm very worried about Mihaela. I was told that I needed to wait two weeks for her to call me."

"Don't worry; she will call you."

"I want her to come to London and meet us, and that's what I'm going to tell her."

"She might not be able to answer. She has a very sensitive security job in Washington, but let's try to contact her. It's not going to harm her."

The next morning, Mihaela received a message from her brother.

"He is anxiously waiting to talk to me and give me 'incredible news.'"

I decided it was safe to answer and wrote back, "I'm well, talk to you soon." I didn't want to say anything else. Tomorrow, I will call him from Bucharest. I received a note from Hamid to go to the meetings with the rest of the group, and he would see me for lunch. I need to tell Rafael that I am meeting Hamid later. During breakfast he gave me a small paper saying, "I'm invited too."

The mood on the bus was happy since today would be the last day in Iran. Everything was extremely boring. They were bored with the lectures, the food, and everything that was prohibited. No movies, no alcoholic beverages, zero entertainment. This is not what they expected. It was a trip for two weeks of anti-American rhetoric. That's what was proclaimed. The guide, who we knew was a government operative, reported the disappointed conversation and conclusions, but we were going home, and that was what mattered. Foreign delegations were always glad to get out of Tehran.

Lunchtime was at one o'clock, but an official car came asking for me and Rafael. We were taken to the office of the Ministry of Defense. Here Hamid greeted us and told us we would meet his brother. He then told Rafael that the minister of petroleum would offer him that job, and he advised him to accept it. "I'll be your boss, and I will treat you like a king," he added. Hamid's brother was very cordial, and surprisingly he gave me his hand to shake. He was as tall as his brother, but unlike him, he was handsome and had a friendly smile. I could tell he had an excellent personality.

The petroleum minister received Rafael alone. He was a man of a few words. "Hamid recommended you. How much do you make in Romania?"

"I make two hundred and fifty thousand per year, have three weeks' vacation, and get a special bonus for my special abilities."

"OK, I can double everything you just said for the first year, and if your drilling abilities are proven, I can triple everything."

"I need to travel frequently to visit my family."

"No problem. You do your job, and you can come and go freely. Do we have a deal?"

"I have a contract."

"I'll give you a month to consider." He gave me a hand-shake and left me his private telephone number. I recorded everything and sent it. We then had lunch with Hamid and five other VIPs. They spoke in Farsi, so although Mihaela was attentive, I played around with my iPhone. I took some pictures of my interesting surroundings. I was then dispatched back to my group.

Mihaela was escorted to a different car. It took her to the hotel. She got a message on the way. One word: Bathroom. She went to the bathroom.

That was strange, Hamid was overly careful now. What was happening?

CHAPTER 77

FINALLY!

A refreshing openness existed now between Loana and Joko. That night, all they did was talk and kiss, and they fell asleep in Joko's room. The excitement was supreme. She had thanked her boss, Mr. Tomasso, and his family, and they reserved their flight to London for early the next day. This time they were going to fly first class. Joko's father was going to kill his son. He had gone overboard and spent €12,000 on a diamond ring at the hotel's jewelry shop. He wasn't afraid. One of the automaker companies had offered him $500 million for 10 percent of the stock in a company that hadn't been formed yet. They knew that his invention was a reality but had no concrete evidence that it would function as he described it. He could have been another person with a scheme, but their engineers told them differently. Constantin called Joko, and was sent sufficient information about the project so they could program the best way to handle the future enterprise. That was going to be the job of his future brothers-in-law. Joko reassured them that he wanted them as equal partners, and he wanted Mihaela included. It was difficult for them to believe him. In their eyes, Joko was only a small-shop auto mechanic. Now, he was offering them partial ownership of a great invention. They were given the flight number and were very happy with the decision to return immediately to London.

They all seemed to be worried about Mihaela. All wished they could have her meet, so they could be together and celebrate. In fact, Loana had called her parents and told them to fly to London to participate in the reunion and celebration. Concerning Loana, the plan is to let her brother and Dimitru take care of the family business. Joko and Loana decided to get married and go on a honeymoon, and there was no need to make any other plans. They felt they had missed a lot of time by not being together sooner. Let Constantin's plan for success for the entire family now become a reality. Only Mihaela was the missing link.

Mihaela got her backpack ready as instructed by the group guide and was ready to leave her room when she received a message from Hamid: I need to talk. Hamid wanted to meet her before she left the hotel for the airport. His absence yesterday was strange, unlike his behavior of the last two weeks. When she went down to the garden, she saw a changed Hamid. His pride and personality had received some type of blow. A tear flowed out of his eye; he was definitely sad. She could tell that he did not have good news. The first thing he did was ask to see her phone. He went to where she stored her photos and didn't find anything there. "What happened to the selfies we took?" "I tried to look for them and accidentally erased everything. I was going to tell you that, but yesterday you didn't call me." "Oh, thank God they disappeared! Look, Mihaela," he said, grasping her hand, "I have a new situation now that my brother knows of my feelings for you. He asked me to put a stop to that immediately. I cannot marry a non-Muslim. My intentions were very serious. If I marry you, my family will suffer untold consequences. My brother's very important position would disappear. He is now a candidate for president. His opponents would have a field day. I'm so sorry I led you on. I really have intense feelings for you, but for your safety and mine, I must say goodbye." Mihaela was able to appear emotional, and tears came down her cheeks, proclaiming disappointment. She said in a whispering voice that she understood and asked him to visit or call her. He told her that he would remain in touch with her. She also told him that she would miss his promise to be with her in London. "I will see you there. I promise to try, but remember, I can't marry you. I can only wish things were not this way in the world." With that, he gave her a hug and quickly left because he could not control his disappointment and sadness.

Mihaela had placed the phone on record and sent out the message. She was sad also. This "feared by all" man had become as tame as a lamb and really taught her a lesson concerning the effect a woman could have on any man. As she projected forward, she felt a shiver of fear for the possible consequences when the agency tried to recruit him with the evidence that she helped them gather. His anger, hurt, and disappointment might explode at that point. It was betrayal. There was nothing she could do to prevent his hurt and anger. This was her mission, and she had accomplished it. She was learning just how rough world politics were. She sent a message to Radu: I will call from Bucharest.

After her arrival in Bucharest, Mihaela was a changed woman, now an independent salary earner who did not have to be maintained economically by anyone. Mihaela had experienced the love of two men, and completed her first mission with resounding success. She knew the power, and danger, of her femininity. Now back in Bucharest, she called her father, but discovered that her parents were in London. For the next few minutes, her father gave her a report of everything that had happened in such a short time. Being out of touch she was now being given the news of her siblings' experiences and successes, that were beyond belief. Mihaela was so happy Daniela's, Constantin's, and Loana's lives were on the way to happiness and fulfillment in a most conventional way. Constantin's plan, which they had accepted but dreaded all along, was converting into a joyful and loving situation for all of them. Her parents were out of the slums of Bistrita. They wanted her to fly to meet them in London and have the family reunited. They had never been apart for any period of time before this. Shortly after hanging up the phone, Constantin called her. He joyfully repeated everything, not knowing that she had already been told. It was such wonderful news that she just listened silently as he spoke, with tears of joy in her eyes. It was still hard to believe it. Then Daniela took the phone from Constantin and said, "My God, how things have changed! Our dream has become reality." When there was a brief pause after all their good news, they all wanted to know where she was. Explaining that she had just arrived in Bucharest, understandably they wanted her to fly into Heathrow to meet them and reunite the family to celebrate everyone's good news. It was hard to say no; they repeated over and over, "Mihaela, we miss you." She couldn't right now because of her job she needed to be back in Washington. She couldn't tell them where she had been and what was accomplished. As an operative of the US government, she was sworn to secrecy. Her desire was for citizenship for herself and her husband-to-be. Mihaela knew that by her work, she could earn that. When the family members asked if she had met anyone, she told them, "I'm working on that, but I am very busy at work." It was followed by saying that when the right person comes along, she would let them know. Constantin explained that with the impending riches the family would have, she could resign her job and just join the family venture. It was going to be a billion-dollar company. She thanked them for including her and caring for her but told them that right now she had decided to continue the very interesting and motivating job that she had began. This was the first breath of fresh air as a full adult out in the larger world, and it felt very good. Similarly, when Rafael invited her to stay in his apartment, Mihaela decided that at this moment she needed time to think over her life and future. Mihaela thanked him for his good intentions. For the first time, she was in charge, not her father or Constantin. She chose to go to a hotel near the airport and called Radu. Mihaela was asked to return to Washington for debriefing, and was congratulated with "Mission accomplished." She felt proud of herself. She had done so much more than anyone ever expected of her, including herself. Was this success? Mihaela thought so, until she saw her phone with ten missed calls from Hamid.